The Cost of Hope

G. S. Carr

The Cost of Hope

This is a work of fiction. All characters in this publication are fictitious and any resemblance to real people, alive or dead, is purely coincidental.

This edition published in 2018

http://www.gscarr.com/

ISBN-13 978-1719552233

1 2 3 4 5 6 7 8 9 10

To my amazing husband who patiently stood by me while I was up until 3 am some nights bringing this work to life. And to my talented sister from another mister Kenya Davis, whose drive and creativity inspires me to never give up on my art and to keep honing my craft.

Chapter One

New Brockton, Alabama
Spring 1867

SARAH STARED INTO THE coffin-sized hole that represented the end of her hope. Mrs. Williams was dead,
and with her had died the little protection she'd provided.

Rain poured down, plastering Sarah's dress to her body
like a second skin. The wind pelted her with droplets of
water, each one an icy razor. She didn't mind the pain; because of it her outside matched the painful bleakness she felt
within.

The storm howled its intent to destroy her, but to Sarah, it
was no more than a mosquito's annoying buzz. She knew she
needed to get out of the storm, but her body refused to move.
All she could do was stare into the black hole and try to keep
the maddening hysteria at bay.

The light pull of a tiny hand on her skirt freed her from
her trance. Air filled her lungs as her chest heaved with a
cleansing breath like a corpse come back to life. Sounds, sights,

and sensations flooded her previously muted brain. Lightning flashed across the gloomy night sky, illuminating the rows of weathered headstones around her. Each told the brief story of a person once amongst the living.

Sarah closed her eyes against the despair lurking at the edge of her sanity. As she opened her eyes, the sight of her beautiful daughter's face was a balm for her soul. This precious little one was the reason she needed to hold tight to her mental stability.

"Maman, come inside."

Sarah stroked the side of her daughter's face. A small smile pulled at her lips. "*Oui mon trésor.* We will catch our deaths in this rain." She allowed Hope to pull her by the hand, silently following her back to the house.

The soft thud of the front door closing as they entered the house sounded like the loud hammer of a nail being driven in her own coffin. A chill ran along Sarah's spine as they walked down the narrow hallway toward their room. She looked over her shoulder to find a set of lustful eyes roaming every inch of her body. Disgust hit her hard, which made it difficult to keep it off her face. She managed to hold tightly to the mask of indifference she had been trained to wear at all times.

James's lewd thoughts were on full display. His hand stroked up and down his inner thigh as his eyes slowly undressed her. His leash had been removed, and for the first time in a long time, Sarah felt petrified. A beating she could take, but to endure what she saw in his eyes...she wasn't so sure. She averted her gaze back to her daughter. She needed to come up with a plan to protect them, and soon.

"Maman he scares me."

Sarah lay next to her daughter in their tiny bed, stroking her pigtails as she held her close. "I know, *mon amour*. But do not worry I will always protect you."

"Promise?"

"Of course, my dear." Sarah kissed her on the forehead and pulled the covers to her chin. "How much do I love you?"

"Five hugs' worth," Hope said. Her little arms opened wide, fingers wiggling.

"How much do I love you?"

"Twenty hugs' worth!"

"How much do I love you?" Sarah whisper-shouted.

"Unlimited hugs' worth!"

"That's right! I love you with all that I am. Now close your eyes and rest."

Hope kissed her mother on the cheek before rolling to her side and closing her eyes. Sarah stroked her daughter's head until her breathing evened out and sleep claimed her. Meanwhile, what-ifs and trying to piece together a plan for their future kept sleep an elusive state for Sarah.

Nightmare became reality when the room door creaked, alerting Sarah to an intruder's presence. The glow of his candle-light cast a sinister look over James's features.

Sarah squeezed her eyes shut and lay perfectly still, willing him away.

"Sarah, come to me now," he whispered into the room.

She refused to move. She prayed to whatever God would listen to a nobody like herself that he would leave her be.

"I said come now, or I'll come get the little brat instead."

"Yes sir."

The rush of nausea at the thought of what was to come nearly sent her rushing for a waste bin. Tears stung the back of her eyes, but she refused to let them fall. She extracted herself from her daughter's arms, slipping from the bed.

The smile of triumph and gloating spread across James's face with each step she took toward him. She locked her hands at her sides to keep from smacking it off. Each step took more effort than the last. Her feet dragged across the floor as though laden with iron. Satisfied that she would follow, James turned to lead the way to his bedroom.

Panic, swift and overwhelming, overtook Sarah as the door to James's room came into view. Her breaths wheezed through her lungs and tiny stars formed at the sides of her vision. Every fiber of her being wanted her to turn and run.

Like a predator taunting its prey, James held his room door open for Sarah to walk through ahead of him. Sarah took one step at a time, each more difficult than the last, until she stood just over the threshold.

James brushed past her to sit in his large wing back chair in the room's corner. Near him, a fire simmered in the fireplace. Under different circumstances it would have lent a soothing, romantic ambiance to the room.

Sarah stole a peek at the large brass, four-poster bed in the middle of the room. No embroidered pillows or other decorations rested on the large surface, only starched white sheets and a serviceable blue spring quilt. She had made that bed three days ago. If she had known it would be the place her soul died, maybe she would have taken more care to add a little beauty to it.

With his legs spread wide, his back slouched against the chair, and his hands clasped together in his lap, James looked every bit the arrogant king of his castle. As if made of stone, Sarah stood unmoving with her gaze trained on the floor, awaiting his next command.

"Come."

It took a moment for Sarah to get her feet to move, but slowly they carried her to stand in front of James. A rough hand gripped the skirt of her dress and pulled her between his open legs.

"You belong to me now. Isn't that right?"

"Yes," she whispered past dry lips.

"My mama treated you too good. Had you thinking you were something special. And them nut-job Yankees went and gave you darkies freedom. Foolishness. Well, my mama is gone, and you're my *employee* now. That means we play by my rules. From now until I say so, you sleep in my bed. You want to sleep in my bed, don't you?"

Sarah couldn't push the lie he wanted to hear past her lips. To some, James might be considered handsome: his sandy blond hair, chiseled jaw, and clear blue eyes were features many envied. But Sarah could see the evil beneath; she saw the darkness that would have him beat her simply for his own amusement. She had seen it first-hand, and his inner ugliness bled right through those blue eyes.

She knew what she needed to say, but couldn't bring her lips to form the words. As the seconds ticked by with the words unspoken, James's lips pressed into a white slash. He dug his fingers into Sarah's waist and squeezed.

"I said you want to sleep in my bed don't you."

She winced in pain but refused to cry out.

"Yes," she ground out past gritted teeth.

"Good." His grip on her waist loosened as he sat back in his chair with a smug grin. "Get on your knees and crawl to me."

"No!" The reaction was so immediate and primal, Sarah couldn't stop the word before it slipped from her mouth. All playfulness vanished from James's face. *Beast. Demon.* These words came to mind as Sarah faced the twisted expression and heinous snarl that overtook his face.

Sarah didn't see it coming until it was too late. James's hand shot out, slapping her across the face. She was too shocked to recover her balance before she crumpled to the ground.

"I said crawl. Now!" James growled. "Or else I'll go get that little brat and play with her instead."

"No! Please, I beg your forgiveness."

Sarah obeyed his command, crawling on her hands and knees to James's chair.

James's hand shot out again, slapping her across the other cheek. She found herself dazed and on her back, the metallic taste of blood pooling in her mouth.

A heavy body came atop her, crushing the air from her lungs. James clawed at her clothing, ripping the fabric and raining wet sloppy kisses over her neck and face.

Fear, thick and crushing, spurred her into action. Fueled by instinct, Sarah clawed, kicked, and fought with everything she had.

She bucked her body as wildly as she could, trying her best to push him off. But his hold was too tight, and her struggling only served to tire her out.

As if restraining a child, James grabbed her small wrists in his large hands and pinned them above her head.

"That's right, fight back. It makes this more fun."

"Get off me!" she yelled.

Despite her exhaustion, Sarah refused to stop fighting. He would not crush her soul. This would not be her fate. She would never be a willing victim. In the only act of defiance left to her, Sarah spit in his face.

James smiled and wiped the spit on her dress.

"Get off my mama!"

Startled by the small voice, Sarah craned her neck to see Hope running toward them.

"No, *mon amour*! Stay back."

The command fell on deaf ears as Hope began pounding on James's back.

As if she weighed nothing, James grabbed the back of Hope's dress and flung her backward.

Tears spilled unchecked down Sarah's face at the sight of her little girl crumpled on the ground, crying. She took advantage of James's distraction, and balling her fists, she put all her strength into the punch she landed under his chin.

He fell back, and Sarah pulled herself from underneath him. She rose to her feet and ran to Hope, scooping her into her arms.

She was halted in her tracks by the burning of her hair being ripped from her scalp. Her head and neck jerked backward, and tears burned the back of her eyes. The pain was so intense she nearly dropped Hope.

"You're gonna pay for that," James snarled, next to her ear.

His hot breath was laced with the acrid smell of tobacco; it assaulted her nostrils, almost caused her to lose the contents of her stomach.

Hope's frightened wails. Searing pain. The overpowering sensory stimuli threatened to shut down her ability to think.

Desperate, Sarah's eyes scanned the room until they spotted the vase perched on the dresser next to them. She reached out with her free hand to grab the vase before swinging it over her shoulder, connecting with James's head.

Almost as soon as she felt the ease of tension in her scalp, a searing pain sliced across her back. Sarah stumbled forward, an arm extended to brace herself against the dresser.

Silence. The deafening drum of her heart and harsh, ragged breathes being pulled into her lungs nearly caused her to miss it. No noise from her attacker greeted her ears. That James had been injured-or worse-was almost too fanciful a thought to hope for.

Trembling racked her body as she glanced over her shoulder. James lay unconscious on the floor. In his hand was his hunting knife, dripping with blood.

Sarah's brain went blank with relief and shock. She momentarily forgot how to speak, how to think, how to move.

Light whimpers penetrated her foggy mind. Sarah looked down at her daughter's tear-streaked face. That Hope had witnessed James's abuse tore a new hole in Sarah's heart. She chastised herself for failing at her most important job of protecting her daughter, no matter the cost.

But such thoughts were for another time; she needed to move. Fueled by the adrenaline surging through her veins, Sarah ignored the pain in her back as she kicked the knife away from James's hand and ran to her room.

Sarah placed Hope on the floor before she scanned the room. What would they need? She would have to hold Hope for most of the journey and wouldn't be able to carry too much extra weight with her wound.

"Maman, I'm scared."

"I know, *mon amour*. All will be well."

"You gots blood there," Hope said, pointing at her mother's back.

"I know, but it doesn't hurt. Grab Mr. Snow."

Without protest, Hope obeyed and ran to retrieve her make-shift doll from the bed.

Sarah grabbed some fabric from her sewing area, tying some around her wound to stunt the bleeding and the rest around her shoulder to create a sling. She packed a bag with thread, scissors, and an extra dress for herself and Hope.

"Come here, my love," she beckoned to her daughter.

Sarah scooped Hope into her arms, then tucked her into the sling. With one last scan of the room to make sure she had what she needed, Sarah turned to walk out the door.

As soon as her feet touched the ground outside the place she had called home for the past six years, Sarah broke into a run.

Where are you going? her mind screamed at her. She had no answer, but she knew she had to keep running. She had to get Hope to safety. The head start she had wouldn't last forever; soon James would wake up and send the dogs after her.

She had to keep running. Just keep running.

Chapter Two

Elba, Alabama

LEX SAT BEHIND HIS large oak desk, staring at the empty frame before him. Minutes ticked by, taking with them pieces of the stress he had accumulated during the day.

Homes needed repairing. Crops needed tending. Disputes needed to be settled. And he was responsible for it all. At the age of five and twenty, he had more wealth than he could ever spend before the burdens of life would take him to an early grave.

Crickets chirped in the yard outside his window as the sun slowly sank behind the trees. He released a deep, calming breath as he closed his eyes to help his mind go blank.

"Hello, old friend."

Alex groaned but kept his eyes closed, ignoring his intruder.

"I'm well. Thank you for asking," his guest said.

Alex opened his eyes to see Charles standing in the doorway of his office. His friend had long since dispensed with personal boundaries, inviting himself over whenever he pleased.

Without invitation, he strolled to the sideboard to pour two drinks before dropping into the chair in front of Alex's desk. He slid one of the two glasses of scotch across the desk to Alex.

Not taking his eyes off his presumptuous friend, Alex took the drink and pushed it to the side.

With a shrug, Charles lifted his in cheers before tossing it down his throat. "As always, I have come to pry you from the clutches of your work. It is officially the end of your day. Virginia has sent me to fetch you to our house for dinner."

Alex picked up his abandoned glass and emptied its contents while he searched for an excuse. He loved Virginia to death, but the woman could smother any man with all her coddling, especially now that she was in the family way. She would barely let him take off his coat before bombarding him with a million questions about his emotional and mental stability.

"I would love to, but—"

"Stop right there. This is non-negotiable. Virginia has made it very clear that returning without you is not an option, and I aim to please my wife."

"Have sympathy on me. I love your wife like a sister, but if she keeps treating me like a mental patient I'm afraid I might actually become one."

"Come now, if I leave you here alone, how will you pass your evening? Staring at the empty frame all night? Or lost in your endless pile of work?"

Alex glanced at the frame in question. A twinge of anger seeped into his heart. He quickly tamped it down, averting his eyes to the empty glass in his hand. Charles meant well, and how could he know what the frame represented? He hadn't shared with a single soul what it meant to him. "Is there any way I could come tomorrow night? As you mentioned, I have an endless mountain of work I need to attend to."

"Absolutely not. Besides, that's all the more reason to take a rest for the evening. You can attack the work well-rested in the morning. And you do know you have a staff of some of the best workers in the state of Alabama? You need to delegate more."

"If I do something myself, I don't have to worry about if it will get done, and done well."

"You need to learn to give up control."

"Maybe so, but that is for another day." Alex moved a stack of papers around on his desk, while pointedly meeting Charles's gaze. It was a facade, as he had no intention of continuing his work that evening, but at least he could attempt to make Charles feel guilty for his intrusion. "As you wish," Alex finally said. "Let us be off, then."

"Marvelous. The carriage is waiting outside."

As he followed Charles through the door, Alex summoned all his patience for the dinner ahead. He would do his best to be a good guest. He truly did enjoy Virginia and Charles's company; he only wished he could enjoy it in more limited doses.

Heat. Bone-melting heat. All Alex wanted to do was run away from the blazing flame. His legs pumping beneath him should have eaten away the distance between him and the flame, but no matter how hard he pushed himself, he stayed rooted to the spot.

The flame danced gracefully behind him, reaching out, calling him to dive into its core. Tired of fighting a losing battle, Alex was tempted to do just that.

As he reached out to accept the offer, bombs fell from the sky, striking the earth around him. Gravel and dirt sprayed his face. Like the roar of a hungry lion, the earth shook and rumbled as it opened and swallowed Alex whole.

He fell down, down, down into a black void of nothingness. There was no sound, no light. All sensory stimuli ceased to exist in this space. Until, like the growing crescendo of an orchestra, her voice rose from the darkness to his ears. First as a dull cry, then a wail of agony. Soleil's screams traveled through his ears straight to his heart. She screamed for help. She screamed his name, but there was nothing he could do. He couldn't find her. He couldn't help her.

Alex opened his mouth to answer her call, but no words could slip past his lips. He was choking, barely able to draw in a breath. Something had lodged in his throat, and he heaved and pressed against his stomach to force it out.

Bullets rained from his mouth, followed by a thick iron chain. Soon these disappeared, and a sound came from his mouth.

But it was not his voice.

Out came his fellow soldiers' cries and screams of agony. Their faces floated before him, surrounding him. Terror, guilt, and sorrow tore at his soul like knives, slicing through his humanity until it seemed there was nothing left.

Alex bolted upright in bed. Sweat poured down his face. Keeping his body perfectly still, he scanned his surroundings for danger. Wardrobe, washstand, pier glass. No soldiers. Slowly his mind brushed off the confines of sleep, reminding him of where he was.

Alex lay back in his pillows and stared at the ceiling. He reviewed his evening, recalling his dinner with Virginia and Calvin to reassure his brain he was not in danger. As his breathing returned to normal, he looked out the window at the moon high in the sky. Its luminous glow kissed the land below it, indicating the time was somewhere between late evening and the threshold of dawn.

In a few hours, he would be expected to take the helm of his plantation, and provide all the answers he didn't feel qualified to give. As he had so many times before, Alex left his room and headed for the stables. Sleep was no longer an option. His brain would not voluntarily allow him to reengage with his demons. On nights such as these, riding soothed his frayed nerves enough to help him function the next day.

Alex breathed in the warm, early morning air as he rode through the woods. The fragrance of fresh spring flowers caressed his nostrils as it floated by on the breeze. Bushes rustled as the nocturnal creatures dashed through the leaves.

Tonight, like many other nights, he headed north toward

the edge of his property. The forest was densely populated with game and scarcely saw people except for the occasional traveling passerby, which made it Alex's favorite hunting location. On nights like tonight, it was also the perfect place to escape the realities of his life.

Alex had been riding for some time when his ears picked up a low rumbling in the distance. As the sound came closer, it transformed into the fast pounding of several horses' hooves, accompanied by the frantic barks of dogs and the occasional yelps of men.

Alex pulled his horse to a stop, waiting until the riders passed by so as not to scare them. Having a bullet pierce his hide because someone mistook him for wild game was not how he planned to end the evening.

As the group came closer, the slender frame of a person emerged, running a slight distance ahead of the herd of riders.

⚜

Sarah ran as fast as she could. Between the gash across her back and the small load in her arms, she moved slowly. To find a river to conceal her scent was a blessing she dared not wish for. Blood flowed from her wound under the strain of her physical exertion, which gave the dogs no trouble keeping track of her.

"Maman, I scared."

Sarah's heart filled with determination on seeing the panic etched across Hope's face. "I will not let you come to any harm, *mon amour.*"

Sarah looked over her shoulder, fear clinging to her like a vice around her heart. James and his men were closing the gap between them with each passing second. She had minutes before she and Hope found themselves captured prey. Despite her brain's primal command to keep moving, Sarah stopped to allow herself time to think.

The slim trunks of the tall, shortleaf pine trees would do little to obstruct her pursuers' view of her. As she examined her surroundings, an idea sprouted in her brain. She ran to the thicket of shrubbery they had passed a few feet back. Sarah untied the sling that had been holding Hope and placed the little girl on the ground.

"Listen to me," she said as she picked up leaves and fallen branches to cover the girl, "I want you to stay here. No matter what, do not come out until the morning. They will be gone by then. Keep walking until you find people. Tell them you are white. Don't ever tell them your mama is a Negro."

"Maman, don't leave me."

Sarah kissed her daughter's wet cheeks. "You are my brave little one. Don't worry, I will always be watching over you."

With one last kiss, Sarah turned and began running again. She ran in the opposite direction of Hope's hiding place, sticking out her hand to rub blood against the trees she passed along the way. The adrenaline pushing her had waned when she stopped, and the intense pain of her wound flooded her system and stole her strength. All she could do was pray, and will herself to put one foot in front of the other.

In a matter of minutes, the two hounds surrounded her, cutting off her escape. Jaws snapped near Sarah's ankles, and barks echoed through the night sky as they waited for their master's command. Ever watchful, her eyes never left the two animals in anticipation of possible attacks.

Soon James and his men rode in behind the yelping dogs. The three men jumped from their horses and joined in the circle of predators surrounding Sarah. An order from James to "heel" cut off the insistent barking. Gone were the vicious beasts, and in their place, tongue-wagging hounds who appeared bored of the entire situation. Sarah tried her best to show no fear as she braced herself for what was to come.

"So you thought you could escape me, did you?" James sneered.

Jaw set, fists balled at her side, Sarah said nothing, staring past him.

"Did you think I would let you get away after that stunt? I'm going to take great pleasure in breaking you. I will teach you your place once and for all. Where is the girl?"

Sarah continued staring past James, not uttering a single syllable.

"I asked you a question, and you will answer me."

She ignored his threat, refusing to answer.

"Have it your way." James pulled back his arm and punched Sarah in the face. Her little frame hurtled to the ground under the impact of the blow. The skin of her cheek tightened in preparation for the bruise that was to follow. Blood seeped between her lips and into her mouth.

She made no attempt to move. She lay on the ground, ready to take the beating he would give her. As long as Hope was safe.

Alex sat atop his horse, watching the scene unfold. He had seen the woman deposit the little girl in her hiding place, and then when the riders finally caught the woman. He was too far away to make out the faces of the people, but he was sure she was a colored woman.

Spurred into action by the blow delivered to the woman, Alex led his horse into a gallop toward the people. It was sickening how some still tried to treat Africans.

"You there, leave her alone!" Alex shouted across the distance.

The three men went rigid before turning to see Alex approach. When they noticed he was alone, each man relaxed, confident in their victory should the situation escalate to violence.

"She belongs to me, and I will do what I want with her. Now keep moving," said the man who had delivered the blow.

Alex opened his mouth to reply but was struck mute by the sight before him. He felt temporarily paralyzed by so many emotions running through him at once. Mouth hanging open, all he could do was stare at the woman. He didn't know if he was experiencing his greatest dream or his worst nightmare.

Breaking free of the spell, he dismounted his horse, taking tentative steps forward. He ignored the men as he walked to the motionless woman on the ground and bent before her. His hand hovered above her, afraid to make contact and find out it was just a hallucination.

"What do you think you're doing?" the ringleader demanded.

The words didn't even register in Alex's brain; he continued staring at the woman before him. "Soleil?"

As if summoned by his greatest wish and deepest desires, here she was. After six years, here Soleil lay before him. What was she doing running from these men? Alex's eyes ran over her body and saw the back of her dress soaked in blood. Her skin had taken on a pale, ashen coloring that worried him as much the blood. She was in desperate need of medical attention. It took everything in him not to pull out his pistol and shoot each man between the eyes.

But what was most concerning to him was the look in her eyes. They were as bleak and devoid of emotion as if he were a stranger, no better than the men chasing her. Why hadn't she spoken to him yet?

"What have you done to her?" he breathed.

"None of your damn business. Now keep moving before I teach you about messing in other people's affairs."

Alex paid no mind to the man's threat. He finally allowed his hand to touch Soleil, and it cut him deep to see her flinch away from his touch. "Soleil, I am going to help you. May I lift you to bring you to my horse?"

For a moment, Alex wondered if she understood his question. Her forehead wrinkled, eyes narrowing; she stared up at him as if he had asked about the composition of the universe. Her eyes darted between him and the man who had attacked her, as though weighing her options. With a nod, she made it clear she thought him the lesser danger.

Alex pulled Soleil into his arms. As he had expected, the men made no move toward him, but instead looked at each other, unsure what to do. Never taking his focus off Soleil, he studied her face. She carried confusion and fear in her eyes. She made no move to push him away, but the stiffness of her body told him she didn't trust him, either. She watched him carefully, taking in every movement without saying a word. There were so many things he wanted to ask her, but he had to get her medical help first.

"Now where do you think you are going with her? She's mine."

"This woman belongs to no man. The law eliminated any claim you had to her years ago, not that you ever had a true claim to her. She was born as free as you and me. I intend to return her to her proper place."

"So you know her? Well I'm sorry, but I don't much care how she was born. She works for me, and I'm not letting her go. Hand her over." James took a step forward with his men close on his heels, as though to intimidate Alex.

Alex looked the man over, then turned his back on him to place Soleil in his saddle.

"Please—my daughter."

Alex faltered; her words hit him like a physical blow. The child was her daughter? She had given birth to the child of another man? A new sadness overtook him. "I saw where she is hiding. I will get her for you."

Alex looked back at the men. "This woman and her child are coming with me, and there will be no debate on the subject. Although you do not deserve it, I am a man of commerce, and I will compensate you for your loss. Come to the Cummings plantation in the morning and we will negotiate the price." Without waiting for a response, Alex pulled on the reins, moving the horse forward.

The men made no attempt to follow. They were rooted to the spot, undoubtedly stunned by who he was. Once they regathered their wits, they would likely think of nothing but the obscene amounts of money they could extract from him.

Satisfied he would not be pursued, Alex concentrated on the frail woman slouched in his saddle. By the grace of God, he had been given a second chance, and he would not squander it.

Alex heard the men mount their horses and ride off as he made his way to collect the little girl.

It was a short distance to her hiding place. The sound of soft whimpering carried to his ears the closer they came to the shrubbery. He pulled back the foliage to uncover the little girl curled in a ball with her legs tucked into her chest. When she looked at him, his heart broke once more. It crushed his soul that so much terror and sadness could reside in someone so small. Her dirty little cheeks were streaked with tears, almost making them clean.

He bent before her but made no move to touch her. "Hello, little one. I will not harm you. I am here to help you and your mother. She is on my horse, waiting for you." He pointed behind him to his horse.

The little girl followed the direction of his finger and looked relieved to see her mother.

Soleil outstretched her arms; she was barely able to whisper, "Hope, *viens chez moi, mon petit.* Everything is fine now."

Hope looked from her mother to Alex, then back to her mother. As instructed, she rose from the ground.

Alex picked her up and placed her in the saddle in front of her mother. He could tell that Soleil was struggling to stay conscious. He grabbed the horse's reins and began guiding them toward his home.

Chapter Three

As soon as the house came into view, Alex began shouting for Joseph, his stable boy.

When they finally reached the house, the boy ambled toward them, rubbing the sleep from his eyes. "Yes sir, what can I do for you?"

Alex handed him the reins before pulling Hope and then Soleil from the saddle. She had passed out on the ride, but even in unconsciousness, she held tight to her daughter. "Go fetch the doctor. Tell him it is an emergency and I need him immediately."

"But sir, it's so early in the morning."

"I don't care. Go for him, and do not return without him."

Joseph glanced curiously at the woman in Alex's arms but did not argue further. He mounted the horse and rode off.

The front doors opened as Alex made his way up the steps. Vivian stood with her hands on her hips, lips pulled into a deep frown. "Why on earth are you making so much..." The sight of Alex's blood-stained shirt, and the limp woman in his arms cut Vivian's sentence short.

"Good Lord! What happened?" Vivian asked as she came closer to assess the pair. Her eyes grew wide as she got close enough to see the unconscious woman in Alex's arms. "Is that–? How?"

Alex cut her inquiry short as he made his way up the porch stairs toward the front door. "There's no time to explain. I have to get her in bed," he said. "When the doctor arrives, send him to my chambers. Take the child and feed then bath her. Bring her to my chambers afterward," he shouted over his shoulder.

"Maman?"

Alex paused to look down at the little girl. Her lips trembled, and tears teetered on the edges of her eyelids.

Alex took a deep breath to calm his frayed nerves. He needed to collect himself and be strong for her. He looked into her watery eyes. "There is nothing to fear, little one. You are safe."

Her tiny blue eyes bounced between Alex and her mother. She couldn't keep from fidgeting as her hands unconsciously rubbed together. "Maman?" she repeated.

Alex dug deep within himself to bring forth a reassuring smile. "She will be better soon. You can come to her after you have eaten and had a bath."

With a slight nod, she gave Alex permission to take her mother away.

Not wishing to waste any more time, Alex continued into the house, leaving Vivian speechless and staring after him.

Alex sat in his office, staring out the window. He saw nothing in particular, lost in his own thoughts. He had been neglecting his work for the last three days, and despite an endless list of things to do, he hadn't been able to accomplish one task in the last four hours. It was driving him crazy, having Soleil unconscious in bed and being unable to wake her. Even immersing himself in work didn't bring with it the normal peace.

Unable to concentrate, he decided it was time to give up. There was no point in forcing himself to stay in his office when there was somewhere else he truly wanted to be. He rose from his chair and walked toward the door.

It was late at night, and everyone had already gone to sleep. Alex walked noiselessly up the stairs. He had given Soleil the suite adjoining his. To minimize the creaking, he slowly opened the bedroom door and slid into the room. He took a seat on the chair beside the bed, his normal place. He had slept there every night to watch over Soleil's recovery.

Alex looked at the two sleeping forms in the bed. Both appeared to be resting peacefully. Hope was curled next to Soleil with her hand on her chest, as if, even in sleep, she needed constant assurance that her mother's heart was still beating.

Hope was just as beautiful as her mother. Her cream skin was only a shade or two darker than his—a stark contrast to her long, ebony curls. Was this what their children would have looked like? Whether their children would have been as light as him or as dark as their mother, he wouldn't have cared, as long as they came from Soleil. With one last look,

27

Alex relaxed back into his chair and closed his eyes.

Soleil slowly stirred as a dull pain crept through her body, pulling her toward consciousness. She attempted to open her eyes, but the land of sleep held her in its strong grip. She had to fight hard to pull herself from its clutches.

She'd been having the dream about the couple she assumed were her parents. Every time, she saw a beautiful African woman who stood with the regal grace of a princess, and a handsome white man with the same blue-green eyes as her own. They appeared to be beckoning her to them with smiling faces and their arms open wide.

As she opened her eyes, the couple began fading to the back of her mind. The same sense of loss she felt each time she woke from dreaming of them, as if something precious had just been taken from her, began to settle in her chest. Having these people cloud her thoughts without being able to fully remember them always felt like a nightmare, no matter how pleasant the dream.

Soleil stuffed her dream and the emotions it evoked to the back of her mind. It was time to focus on the here and now. The cloud of sleep had lifted from her mind, and she realized she was in a place she had never seen before. Her eyebrows squished together as her eyes roamed her surroundings.

She was in a bed in a small room with walls painted a soft yellow. How did she get into a bed? Where was James? How did she get out of the woods? Her mind raced, trying to piece together the puzzle.

Soleil's attention was drawn by the light sound of snoring and the movement of a small body: Hope, who lay snuggled beside her. The little girl seemed content in her sleep as if the world held nothing she feared. Soleil reached out to brush Hope's long hair from her face but froze as a sharp pain sliced through her back. Memories of what had transpired the night she ran came rushing back. James's knife slicing into her back, running through the woods with his dogs chasing close behind, and the man. The one who saved her. She vaguely remembered him lifting her off the ground and saving her from James's beating. Who was he? Why had he saved her?

These thoughts filtered into her mind as her eyes continued their perusal of the small room. A few seconds later, they froze on the man in question, asleep in a chair on the opposite side of the room.

Soleil used the little energy she had in reserve to pull herself to a seated postion. After a deep breath to fortify her resolve, she inched her legs over the edge of the bed. The pain intensified, nearly sending her back into the pillows, but she pushed through it, holding to the bedpost to keep herself upright. She needed to find out what this man wanted from her. He had given her a comfortable bed, treated her wound, and taken care of Hope while she was ill. If she knew nothing else, she knew everything had a price.

She sat on the edge of the bed, observing the sleeping figure. He was a very handsome man. His raven black hair was in need of a cut; it hung low in his face, brushing the tips of his eyelashes. Even in his seated position, Soleil could tell from his long, lean frame that he was tall. The thin cotton shirt he wore hinted at a well-muscled chest.

Heat bloomed in her chest and spread outward. A small gasp escaped her lips as she lifted her fanned fingers to her breast bone. She was attracted to him.

She wondered if her injury had somehow affected her brain. He was a plantation owner, and she a recently freed slave. Everything about her attraction to him was wrong. And yet, as she peered at him through slightly hooded eyes, she couldn't deny it was there, along with a sense of familiarity.

Soleil sat as straight as she could without irritating her wound before loudly clearing her throat.

The man's eyelids fluttered before opening completely. He had mesmerizing clear blue eyes. The haze of sleep on his face gave way to awareness and then... concern?

"It is good to see you have awakened. How are you feeling?"

Soleil watched as he stretched his long limbs, never taking his eyes off her. The rich baritone of his voice was somehow soothing, which unnerved Soleil all the more. "I'm alive, which is a blessing. How long have I been asleep?"

"About three days. The doctor stitched your wound, but it became infected. You had a fever, but it broke this morning."

"And you took care of Hope while I slept?" she asked while watching him, analyzing his every word and action for falsehood.

"Yes. She has barely left your side. This morning it took a cookie and a glass of milk to finally get her to play outside with the other children. But after a few hours she came right back to your bedside."

Soleil sat quietly, dissecting his statement. There appeared to be no falsehood in it. His eyes had even softened when he spoke of Hope.

When she didn't speak again, he opened his mouth to fill the silence. "I had several dresses taken out of my mother's trunk for you. They seem about your size, but I fear they are a bit out of fashion. Soon I will take you into town to purchase new dresses for you and Hope."

"That will not be necessary. I brought a dress for each of us."

"A single dress does not make a wardrobe. I insist." Before she could protest, Alex shifted the direction of the conversation. "May I ask how you came by your wound?"

The question was asked innocently enough, but Soleil stiffened and shifted her eyes to her lap. The answer to that was none of his concern, and she didn't owe him an explanation. Or did she? He had saved her life, but did that warrant rights to the details of her personal misfortunes?

Resigning herself to her answer, Soleil let out a soft sigh. "James cut me with his hunting knife the night I ran. He wanted to take liberties I was not willing to allow him, and he threatened Hope. I fought back. I will do anything to protect my child." Soleil leveled a meaningful stare at him as she made her last declaration.

To her surprise, his face turned beet red and his eyebrows and lips scrunched into a menacing scowl. His chest heaved with heavy breaths she assumed were meant to calm him. She braced herself for the possible storm of his emotions. "I promise you and your daughter are safe here. No harm shall ever come to either of you."

Soleil opened her mouth, but no words sprung forth. He had not been upset at her, but for her? She could only look on in confusion at the strong display of emotion on her behalf.

"Why? Why are you helping me?"

"Because you deserve nothing less from me."

Soleil wrinkled her brow and stared, trying to make sense of his words. "What do you mean?"

"You are Soleil Jacqueline Dufor. Your father is Dominique Dufor. Your mother is a beautiful African woman named Imani."

Flashes of the couple from her dreams began to invade her mind. He was lying—he had to be. Soleil refused to digest his words as truth. "That's not possible."

"Yes, it is. You went missing six years ago. What little I could get from that scum James makes me assume you were kidnapped and suffered some head trauma. I could not remove him from my home fast enough, but during our brief exchange he said his mother purchased you around the time you went missing. She called you Sarah because you couldn't remember who you were."

No matter how implausible they sounded, something in his words rung true in her heart. She always knew she had not been born in captivity. "How do you know my family?"

"Our families are old acquaintances. Our fathers had a business relationship. I guess I should reintroduce myself," he said with a chuckle. "My name is Alexander Cummings, but you may call me Alex. We first met when you were thirteen years old. From the first moment I saw you I wanted to protect you, and it nearly killed me when you disappeared."

Soleil averted her eyes as a blush warmed her cheeks. It would be all too easy to read true compassion in those words. She gathered her composure, reinforcing the guard around her emotions, then found his gaze again. When their eyes met, a moment of silence followed. He seemed to be trying to read her as much as she was trying to read him.

"How do I know what you say is true?" she asked.

He reached toward the ground beside his chair and picked up a frame. As though trying not to scare a skittish mare, he rose from his chair slowly and deliberately, stepping toward the bed to hand her the frame.

"What's this?" Soleil took the offered item and gasped when she saw the image. Tears gathered in her eyes; her mind battled over the reality the photo presented and the only reality she had known.

"That frame has sat empty on my desk ever since you went missing. We took that picture the summer after my first year at university. I was eighteen and you were fifteen. You gave me the framed picture as a birthday present. After you were gone I couldn't stand to look at the photo, so I hid it away in my study, but for some reason I wanted to keep the frame on my desk. Probably as a reminder of what I had lost."

It was too much for Soleil to take in. She tried to process it all, but his words and the picture only awakened a headache at the back of her skull. Tears ran unchecked from her eyes as she stared at a young woman who had her face, but was filled with so much joy, hope, and love. Had there really been a time when she had been so happy? Had she really been so carefree?

Soleil handed the picture back to Alex and swiped at the tears running down her face, unable to handle the emotions raging through her. "What will you do with Hope and me?"

"Soleil..."

"What shall become of us?"

With a sigh, Alex allowed the change in topic. "You are free to do as you wish. In light of the mockery the States have made of the 13th Amendment, it will probably be best for you to return to France. You are free on paper, but not in fact. I will inform your parents of your return, and..."

"No!"

Alex's brows furrowed in confusion as he stared at Soleil. She knew she had taken him by surprise with her sudden panicked outburst.

"What? I don't understand."

"Do not inform my parents you have found me."

"Why wouldn't you want your parents to know where you are and that you are safe?"

"Look at me. I am a mangled shadow of the girl in that picture. How could I face them in my current state? They lost a beautiful, innocent girl, and I cannot bear to give them back a scared and broken woman."

As soon as the words left her lips, Soleil wished she could call them back. She hadn't meant to allow that glimpse into her soul. The heartbreak was etched across Alex's face; the corners of his lips pulled down in a severe frown, and sadness shone in his eyes. He looked as if the only thing keeping him from scooping her into his arms and whispering that the bad days were behind her until she felt it in her bones was his fear of her reaction.

With a nod, he agreed. "As you wish."

Her fingers pinched and released the fabric of her nightgown. "Can I call on the friendship we once shared with a request?" She could feel his eyes intent on her. She hadn't fully decided whether asking him for anything was a good idea, but the situation left no choice but to take a small step of faith.

"Never be afraid to ask me anything."

"Will you allow us to stay here with you? Only for a short time, until I can figure out a plan and obtain employment."

"You are a welcomed guest in my home for as long as you would like to stay."

Soleil closed her eyes, basking in the relief that statement brought. When she opened them again, her face was painted with gratitude and determination. "Thank you. I will help around the house to make up for the room and board."

"Nonsense! You owe me nothing."

"I could not take from you without contributing or giving some kind of payment."

Soleil watched as he thought over her statement. For a moment, old fears surfaced as she thought of the alternative forms of payment he might request of her. She slouched a little, clutching the neckline of her nightgown.

"We will discuss what chores you can do in the morning. For now, you should rest. How is the pain?"

"You can probably see how weakened I have become during this exchange, so there is no sense in lying to you. The pain is fairly intense."

Alex reached for a glass on the nightstand and placed it in Soleil's hands. "Here, drink this. The doctor said it will help with the pain and help you rest."

Soleil only hesitated for a moment before bringing the glass to her lips. Once the contents were gone, she handed the empty glass back to him. "Thank you."

"You are most welcome." Alex rose from his chair and turned toward the door. "My suite adjoins this room. Do not hesitate to call if you need anything else. Good night."

"Thank you. Good night."

As she watched him leave the room, Soleil was surprised to feel a deep sense of loss settle over her. She would have to be careful about taming the emotions he evoked in her. She lay back on the bed, pulling Hope close to her as she drifted back to sleep.

Chapter Four

IVIAN HURRIED UP THE stairs toward Alex's office. She had come seeking answers about what he would do with that woman. Vivian had half hoped she would die from her wounds, but unfortunately, the girl awoke early in the morning.

She knocked once and entered before Alex had time to answer. Alex sat behind his desk, reviewing several documents. He looked up when she came in and smiled as she sat in the empty chair in front of his desk.

"What are you going to do with her?" Vivian asked. Under different circumstances she would have been more tactful in her delivery, but this was too important. Even the hard set of his jaw and stiff posture didn't sway her.

"Soleil and her daughter will be staying with us until she has made other arrangements or is ready to return home. She wishes to repay my hospitality by doing a little housework. I will not allow her to lift a finger in my home, so if she asks you to help, send her to find me."

Vivian couldn't fight the gasp that erupted from her lips. He was daring to allow her to stay. She wanted to fan herself against the heat and flush consuming her body, thinking of the scandal of it all. "What?! She can't... You can't... This cannot happen! She must leave at once."

"This is not negotiable," Alex said, slamming his hand on his desk. "This is how the situation will be handled."

"You would ruin your reputation? Throw away the business your father built from nothing—for her? You cannot throw away everything for that Negro woman!"

"My father is dead now, and this is my business. I will worry about what happens, and you will mind what you say about her. I will not tolerate you tearing her down, and you would be wise to remember that. Do I make myself clear?"

Unable to speak over her indignation at being scolded, Vivian nodded once. Without another word, she rose and walked out of the room. But this was far from over.

"You there," Vivian called to the little boy walking toward the stable. "What is your name?"

"Joseph, ma'am," he answered with his eyes cast to the ground.

"I have a task for you, Joseph. You are to deliver this note to the address on the envelope. You are to tell no one what you are about, is that clear?"

"Yes, ma'am," he replied shaking his head vigorously.

"If anyone finds out about this letter, Joseph, there will be hell to pay. For you and your family. Mr. Cummings may own this plantation, but I rule it. Understood?"

"Yes, ma'am." The boy cowered.

"Good. Now off with you. The walk will take you several hours, and I want it delivered tonight."

Without another word, the boy took off running. Vivian watched as he dashed down the road, not even stopping to reply to the few greetings offered by those he passed.

Satisfied, Vivian walked back toward the house.

Soleil sat on her bed, braiding Hope's silky black hair into a single plait down her back.

Miss Eliza stood in the doorway, waiting for her to finish so she could take Hope to play. Apparently, while Soleil recovered, Hope had become fast friends with Miss Eliza and her grandchildren. Soleil could understand why. She had smooth, dark skin like a starless night that made her eyes seem brighter and happier. Her joyful face held a smile as sweet as the cookies she was known to give out. Her ample girth gave children a warm, soft cushion to curl up on and feel protected by.

"Are you sure it isn't an imposition for Hope to join you today?"

"Not at all, miss. My grandbabies love her. They can't wait to play."

A bittersweet smile spread across Soleil's lips. She couldn't remember a time when Hope was out of her sight for an extended period of time. It tore her heart in two to let Hope play without her supervision. She didn't doubt the woman would do her best to keep Hope safe, but it was still so hard. "Thank you again for taking such good care of her while I slept."

"Of course, ma'am. But it was a joint effort. Mr. Cummings lent a helping hand as well."

"Yes he did, Maman. He gave me cookies!" Hope added to the conversation. She nearly poked Soleil in the eye as she thrust three wiggling fingers in her face. "He gave me this many."

"Well that was nice of him," Soleil said with a chuckle.

"He is very nice."

"I can vouch for that," Miss Eliza said with her chest puffed out like a proud mother boasting about her son.

"That is wonderful to hear. Then he is a, um..." Soleil hesitated, fidgeting with the end of Hope's braid. "He's a gentleman, I presume."

Miss Eliza's eyes softened with knowing sadness. "You and your daughter are safe, love. No harm will come to you under Mr. Cummings' watch. I came to live here after you disappeared, but I've heard the stories. The little brown French girl with a fiery spirit that captivated young Mr. Cummings' heart. You are like a legend to some of the people here," she said with a chuckle. "You know, even after slavery ended and we could choose for ourselves, we still stayed."

"Yes, as did I."

"But we stayed because we wanted to. If you put in a hard day's work, you get a fair day's wage and everything you need to take care of your family. Did you have that with your old master?"

Soleil squirmed in her seat. Clearing her throat, she said, "Yes well, thank you for telling me that. It does give me a bit of peace."

"Of course."

Soleil finished Hope's braid, then tied a ribbon to the end before kissing her cheek. "Done. You be good today. Listen to everything Miss Eliza tells you."

Hope slid off the bed before Soleil could even finish the sentence. "Yes, Maman."

She ran to Miss Eliza, grabbing the woman's hand and pulling her toward the door. "Maybe Alex will come and play with me again today."

"His name is Mr. Cummings. And maybe he will."

"No, Maman. He said his name is Alex."

"Mr. Cummings. *C'est claire*?"

"*Oui*, Maman."

"Good. Now go have fun."

Hope didn't need to be told twice. Without another glance in her mother's direction, Hope dragged Miss Eliza out the door.

Alone, Soleil took a moment to reflect on her situation. She still found it hard to believe everything that was happening. This morning a bath had been drawn for her, and she had marveled at the luxury. When Mrs. Williams was alive she had only allowed Soleil the occasional basin of cold water to stay clean, and even then it was only so she wouldn't make the older woman ill.

Washed and wearing a new dress, Soleil felt the best she had in a long time. The doctor had returned earlier that morning and given her a clean bill of health. She was instructed not to do anything strenuous so as not to irritate her stitches. Alex had come in after the doctor left to inform her that, if she needed anything, he would be making his rounds around the plantation. After an awkward exchange of goodbyes, he left her to spend the day as she pleased.

She had a lot to thank Alex for. No matter what his intentions, she knew he could never be as horrible as the man she had escaped. In a moment of honesty, she allowed herself to admit it would be nice to be desired by a man like him. She wondered what it would feel like to have his lips kiss hers. Would they be as soft and gentle as they looked? Had she been kissed by those lips in her youth?

Despite her fantasies, she knew no meaningful relationship could exist for the two of them. With James, she knew what he was and what he was capable of so that she was always able to protect herself. Alex was a different story. She had a feeling that if he made it past her defenses, she might be left broken in the end.

With Hope taken care of, Soleil left her room to search out Miss Vivian. Alex had mentioned she had been his governess in his youth and stayed on with the family as their housekeeper. Soleil wanted to find out how she could help around the house. She could sense that Alex had avoided allowing her to do anything, but she wanted to contribute in some manner.

A spiral staircase brought her to the main level's foyer. To her right lay a sitting room, ornately decorated with the trappings of wealth. Sheer white curtains covered the floor-to-ceiling windows. Floor-length, heavy velvet draperies with tasseled tiebacks rested on top. A sofa, love seat, and armchair surrounded a tea-table made of rich, dark wood with intricately carved leaf patterns. To the left was a formal dining room. She marveled at the intricate design of the crystal chandelier hanging over the long mahogany table.

Behind the staircase was a long hallway. Soleil continued her exploration down the hallway and was pleasantly surprised to find the walls lined with portraits. She stopped to examine each one. The people depicted must have been Alex's ancestors. Each peered out from their frames, looking every bit the aristocrats they probably were. Some held expressions of joy, while others looked as if they would rather be doing anything other than standing to have their features immortalized.

The echo of footsteps alerted Soleil that someone drew near. She stood in the middle of the hall, eyes trained in that direction. When Alex rounded the corner and saw her, a charming grin spread across his face.

At the sight of him, Soleil's lips parted with a slight intake of breath. His sculpted face possessed just enough masculinity to make it handsome instead of beautiful. His clear, sky blue eyes crinkled at the corners like a man who often indulged in laughter. His ebony hair still hung a little too long in the front.

Soleil fought the urge to reach out and brush the offending hairs into place. It seemed like a natural reaction, as if she had done it many times before.

His shirt sleeves were rolled to his elbows, showing off his strong forearms. The top three buttons were undone, revealing a hint of the curly black hair beneath. It was as if his current appearance was meant specifically for her. Alarm bells rang in her head as the war between what she knew and what she felt raged within her.

"What a delightful surprise meeting you here," he said. "Please excuse my disheveled appearance. I was helping mend a fence on the northern side of the property."

Soleil allowed her eyes to sweep over him one last time. "I was just on my way to find Ms. Vivian. I wanted to ask what my chores would be. I stopped to look at the paintings."

"What do you think of them?"

Soleil glanced at the nearest painting, noting that Alex had ignored her comment about chores just as she had ignored his comment about his appearance.

"They are well done. Some are very lovely."

"Thank you."

Soleil watched as Alex crossed his arms over his strong chest, and couldn't keep her eyes from following. She fought the blush she felt creeping up her neck, quickly averting her eyes to a nearby picture.

"The gallery is my favorite part of the house. Something about being surrounded by those who came before gives me peace and the strength to carry on each day. I guess I want to be a part of the legacy that makes them proud."

"I understand. Hope gives me strength. I wake up each morning for her. One day I want to be someone she can be proud of."

"You already are. All she talked about while you were asleep was how great of a mother you are."

As wonderful as his words were, receiving such high praise was foreign to her. Soleil didn't know what to do with it. "Thank you. For everything. You truly saved our lives. I could never repay you for that."

Alex's eyes softened. "Your thanks are gladly accepted."

"Which is your favorite?" Soleil asked with a smile.

Alex's eyes flickered down to her lips, then back to her eyes. "Pardon?"

"The paintings. Which is your favorite?"

He focused his attention on the pictures hanging on the wall, then back at her. "The one of my father." Alex pointed to a man seated in a chair, looking out an open window. He held a look which could have been concentration or concern. The light from the open window illuminated his silvery hair.

"It is a well-crafted piece."

"Would you like to know what he is looking at?"

Soleil could hear the hint of teasing in his voice. "Yes, do tell."

"He was watching me raise cane as a boy. I think I almost burnt down the entire cotton crop the year that picture was done. He told me he had a head of hair as black as mine until I was born. I placed every gray hair upon his head."

Soleil couldn't help but giggle imagining him as a little boy terrorizing his father. At the thought, something tickled the back of her mind. Flashes filtered in: a young man with black hair chasing a girl with caramel skin through the woods. Was it a memory? A dull ache started behind her eyes. To stunt the pain, she pressed her thumb and ring finger into her eyebrows at the edge of her eye sockets.

45

Concern shown in Alex's eyes as he watched the sudden souring of her mood. Soleil opened her mouth to reassure him she was fine, but he beat her to it. "*Quelle est celui que tu aimes le plus?*"

Soleil looked at Alex, stunned. "You can speak French?" Soleil's eyes lit up; another person with whom she could share such a connection! "How did you learn?"

"You taught me. Well, what little I know I learned from you."

Soleil thought about what that meant. They must have spent a significant amount of time together at some point. Were they really such good friends as he claimed?

"*Il est agréable d'entendre quelqu'un d'autre parler ma langue,*" Soleil replied.

The look of confusion on Alex's face told Soleil he didn't understand. Maybe she had been a little overzealous in her joy and spoken too fast.

She repeated her sentence in English. "It is nice to hear someone else speaking my language. I have not shared the ability with anyone except Hope for several years. I taught her so we could communication without Mrs. Williams knowing what we said. Having this connection with someone else will be nice."

"I am pleased you feel that way, but I warn you my French is very limited. I have not used it in quite some time. However, if you are willing to help me again, I will be glad to be your pupil." Alex smiled at her. It was a small gesture, but Soleil admitted that it meant a lot to her. To have someone think she was worthy to teach them anything was new and exhilarating.

It might even be fun to teach him.

"How old is Hope?" he asked.

"Five years of age."

"Who is her father?"

All amusement vanished from Soleil's body. Her eyes narrowed, and she gazed at him suspiciously. "Why do you wish to know?"

"Is it James?"

Soleil swallowed hard as the color drained from her face. Back rigid, she lifted her chin in the air as she tucked her heart behind its carefully erected wall. "Does it matter? The man took what he wanted without consent, and cared not for the destroyed lives he left b ehind. That is the way of you men here, is it not? You do as you please without..." Soleil reined in her emotions and cut off the rest of her r ant. Her sharp tongue had been the cause of many of the punishments she'd received in the past.

To her surprise, he said nothing in reply. No shouting back, no cursing or threats about what was to be her fate. In fact, he looked hurt.

Not wishing to see if that would change, Soleil backed away. "If you will excuse me, I need to get some air."

She was glad when he made no attempt to stop her as she rushed past him. He was too much. The emotions he invoked in her were too much. She needed a plan for her and Hope's future. And soon.

Chapter Five

A COOL BREEZE CARESSED Soleil's skin as she peered at
Alex from behind the wide trunk of a tree. He stood
on the porch of a small cabin, talking with an older
African man who rocked back and forth with the slow, easy
movements of someone who had nowhere else to be.

His arms hung over an axe draped across his shoulders.
A howl of laughter pealed through the air as they shared
an amusing moment. The two men shook hands before Alex
walked down the porch stairs and onto the worn path between
his tenants' small cabins.

With a deep breath to gather her courage, Soleil stepped
from behind the tree and trotted toward Alex. "Mr. Cummings."

Alex halted, turning to face Soleil and waiting as she approached.

As she took in his blank expression, she stumbled a bit, losing confidence in her plan. But she had come with a purpose,
she reminded herself. Gathering her skirts and straightening
her spine, she strode forward with renewed confidence until
they were face to face. "I wanted to apologize for earlier. You
have done so much for me and Hope, and my behavior was

ungrateful and rude. It was uncalled for, and unacceptable. For that I apologize."

"Your apology is not necessary. My questions were intrusive. I should not have asked."

"Yes, James is Hope's father. He..."

"No." Alex raised a hand to cut off the rest of her sentence. "You don't have to tell me any more. In fact, I must admit I do not wish to hear the rest of the story."

"Again, I apologize." Soleil kept her hands clasped in front of her, head bowed and eyes on the ground.

"Look at me." Maybe she was imagining it, but his voice held a note of irritation.

Soleil lifted her eyes to do as he said.

"Once, you called me every mean name you could think of because of how I treated a baby calf. I deserved every name you called me and then some. As I sat listening to you put a sailor to shame, I don't think I could have been more in awe of you. You were so passionate in your righteous indignation, and all for a cow. But that was who you were. Willing to come to the aid of any creature, no matter how insignificant others thought them to be."

With the fluid grace of a lazy southern river, Alex lifted his hand and tucked a loose strand of hair behind her ear. She couldn't control her body's slight flinch as his hand reached out to her, but she did not cower from his touch. "Never apologize to me or anyone else for being who you are. If anyone should apologize, it should be me. I can only imagine the pain and suffering you must have endured these past few years. It is an excruciating torture to know that my little flower had to blossom amongst thorns. My greatest sorrow is that I was not there to shield you from it. I failed you in the most basic way. The night..." Alex choked on the words. "The night you disappeared, I should have stayed with you. That's what a man does for the woman he loves."

Soleil didn't realize tears had fallen from her eyes until Alex's thumb wiped away the moisture from her cheek. "I don't... I don't know what to say."

"You don't need to respond. I know you don't remember me or us, but not a day has passed that I have not loved you. Your passion, your sacrificing heart, even your temper are all part of the wonderful woman you are, and I would not change any of it."

Soleil's heart began a rapid, erratic beat in her chest. Everything in her screamed that this wasn't true, that he could not really love her. Yet, looking into his eyes, she saw only truth. Fear and hope warred for control inside her. Did she dare believe his words and the truth shining in his eyes? What would such belief cost her?

"It is okay if you do not believe me. One day I will prove myself to you. I simply feel blessed that I have been given a second chance." Alex stepped back to give Soleil space. "And as my first order to win your favor, I have a very special surprise for you. You will receive it tonight at dinner."

"A surprise? I... What..."

"You shall see soon enough. Now, I have a few more tenants to see to. Please go and enjoy the rest of the day. I know Hope would love for you to join in her play."

Soleil cleared her throat to help regain control of her voice.

"Before you leave, I also wanted to speak with you about my chores."

"You are barely recovered from a very serious wound. Please do me the favor of resting."

"Why do I have a feeling you are simply trying to placate me, and have no intention of allowing me to contribute to the household?"

Alex smirked. "Because apparently, despite your lapse in memory, you still know me very well. Besides, I have a feeling that one day you will be a very important, contributing member of this household—in different ways."

Soleil did not mistake the meaning of his words. She had seen desire in a man's eyes, and his were ablaze with it. For a moment she allowed herself to think about what it would be like to be swollen with his child, standing by his side as his wife. But just as quickly she tamped the fantasy down.

Breaking their locked gaze, Soleil took a step backward. "Yes, well in that case, I will not press the subject. I will go check on Hope."

"Excellent. I know she will enjoy it. And maybe you will tire her out enough that I only have to be a pony once tonight."

"If she is ever too much..."

"Never. It is truly my pleasure to spend time with her. I will see you both at dinner tonight."

Soleil mustered a small smile. "Yes, we will see you then." She turned on her heels and walked toward the door to search out her daughter as thoughts of what she would wear to dinner floated through her mind. She had the unshakable urge to look her best tonight.

Soleil and Hope walked down the stairs hand in hand. She touched her hair for the millionth time to check that all her curls were still in their proper place. She had pulled them into a single braid tied off with a ribbon. It was a simple hairstyle that did not live up to the grandeur of her beautiful evening gown, but it was the best she could do. She often found herself wondering why on Earth she had never learned to take care of her own hair in her youth. What had stopped her from learning such a vital skill? The mere thought of fixing her hair sent chills down her spine.

Satisfied her hair was as it should be, she ran her hand down her gown to smooth the nonexistent wrinkles. Caring about her appearance was a new—and not all that pleasant—feeling. Why did she care what Alex thought of her? She knew why, but wouldn't admit it, even to herself. Instead, she allowed herself to believe she wanted to show appreciation for his gifts.

When she had come back to her room from playing with Hope, two beautiful aqua blue dresses had been laid across her bed, one a miniature replica of the other. At first she was so stunned, she stopped in her tracks.

It wasn't until Hope ran into the room squealing with joy that she was able to come to her senses. "Look, Maman. Look! My dress is so pretty. Did Alex give them to us?"

The excitement pouring from her daughter was contagious, and Soleil found herself wanting to laugh. She didn't even want to risk dampening her daughter's joy by correcting the way she addressed Alex. "Yes, *mon amour*, he did."

"Can I wear it now?"

Soleil reached to pick up her own dress and saw the note lying next to it. It read, *Please wear to dinner.* "You can wear it at dinner tonight. We must first bathe so that we do not ruin the pretty dresses with dirt."

"I don't want to ruin my dress," Hope said in distress. "Bath now, please."

Soleil couldn't help but laugh at her daughter's exuberance. She had never been so willing to bathe before. But then again, it probably wasn't as much of an imposition now that they could take warm baths in the slipper tub instead of the cold wash-downs at the basin that they were used to. Not wanting thoughts of the past to dampen the cheer of the moment, Soleil pushed them aside to begin the process of making Hope and herself presentable.

<hr />

Alex stood outside the closed dining room doors, waiting as they approached. Soleil immediately noticed how handsome he looked in his evening finery. As soon as Hope saw him, she pulled free of her mother's grasp and ran up to him, arms wide. With little effort, Alex caught her in his arms as she launched herself at him.

"Thank you for my pretty dress. I love it."

"You are most welcome. I am glad you like it. It is a beautiful color on you. Both of you," he said as he turned his smile from Hope to Soleil.

Soleil couldn't help the slight blush that spread across her cheeks. Unable to meet his gaze, she concentrated on her clasped hands in front of her. "Thank you. The dresses are quite beautiful, and I greatly appreciate your generosity. But I am curious why we are so formally dressed for a simple dinner at home."

"In honor of your return I have organized a wonderful surprise, and I am sure you will want to look your best when you receive it. Come now, let us not delay any longer."

Alex threw the doors wide open, stepping aside for Soleil to proceed him. She stepped inside, her eyes roaming the room until they landed on a couple standing in front of the ornate wooden dining table. The woman had a fiery crop of red hair and a face that seemed familiar and yet unknown to her.

An audible gasp escaped the woman's lips. "It is you!"

Soleil watched in slight dismay and simultaneous amazement as the woman, who was very visibly with child, waddle-ran toward her. Soleil closed the distance between them so the woman didn't have too far a journey to make. Within seconds, Soleil found herself crushed between an ironclad grip and a protruding belly.

"It is you! I know Alex would never lie to me, but I just couldn't believe it! But it is you, right here in my arms again! What happened? Where have you been? How did you come back? What—"

"Dearest, how about one question at a time?" the man with her said.

"Right," the woman said with a sheepish grin. "Sorry about

that. I just can't believe it."

The woman looked at Soleil with so much joy and love it almost broke her heart. So many wonderful emotions filled her face when she looked at Soleil, but no matter how much she wished she could, Soleil couldn't return the feelings.

"It brings me great sorrow to have to ask this, as you seem to know me so well, but what is your name?"

Another gasp sprung from the young woman's mouth. She looked in confusion over Soleil's shoulder toward Alex, then back at Soleil. "Do you really not know me?"

"I'm sorry. I do not know how much Alex has told you, but it would appear that during my abduction I lost my memory."

The young woman's hand flew to her mouth as her eyes widened. "My goodness! No wonder you never found your way home. You must have so many questions. Well, let's start with the basics. My name is Virginia. We were the best of friends as young ladies. That tall glass of hot milk over there is my husband Charles," she said with a smile. Soleil couldn't help but laugh at the outlandish description.

At the mention of his name, Charles gave a slight bow. "It is a pleasure to meet you, Soleil. You are a legend in our home, and it is wonderful to finally be able to put a face to a name."

"It is a pleasure to make your acquaintance as well."

"I hate to interrupt," Alex said, "but how about we continue this conversation over dinner? The little miss has informed me she is quite famished."

"Of course! My goodness, you have a daughter? I have so many questions. Let us sit." Virginia wrapped her arm around Soleil's and steered them toward the dining room table. They sat down with Alex at the head of the table, Soleil on his right and Hope on his left. Virginia sat next to Soleil, with Charles directly across.

As soon as everyone was seated, the servers came forward to serve the meal. Soleil gave a nod and small smile of thanks as her plate was placed in front of her. It was still so odd to have someone serving her. For as long as she could remember, she had been the servant who was barely noticed and never heard. No sooner had Soleil picked up her fork than Virginia resumed her inquisition, staring expectantly at Soleil. "So, what has your life been like these past five years?"

Soleil looked longingly at the lovely meal in front of her, then sighed in acceptance; answering questions would be the main activity during this dinner. Garlic and a hint of something else—rosemary, perhaps—danced in her nostrils. It would probably be a while before she tasted it. Her stomach gave a gentle grumble, letting her know it would like to be satisfied.

She placed her fork down to give Virginia her undivided attention. Conversations such as these were always best to face head-on and be done with. "I will try to give you as much detail as possible while being brief."

"No, my dear. Take as much time as you need." Virginia placed her hand over Soleil's in a reassuring gesture. "I want to know everything."

With a glance to her left, Soleil could see Alex's attention focused on her. It seemed he was curious to hear her story as well.

"Well, all I can remember is waking up to the sound of

gruff voices. I now know they were the men who abducted me, bartering with a slave trader. I was sold at auction to an elderly woman, Mrs. Williams. She wasn't a nice woman, but she wasn't overly harsh, either. She doled out what she felt was justice, which included the occasional whipping, but not senseless torture. Due to my ability to read, write and keep books, I ran her house as she became feeble. Mrs. Williams was not a wealthy woman, so it was just her and me along with an older slave, Mr. Jones, that she occasionally borrowed for hard labor. I cooked, cleaned, cared for the animals, and tended her small crop. She always made sure I had enough to take care of myself and Hope, whom I acquired along the way."

Soleil paused to look lovingly at her daughter. Hope barely noticed as she tucked into her meal. "Mrs. Williams died in her sleep. That is how I found myself in James's care, and with the need to run. For the sake of sensitive company, I will simply say he was no gentleman, and refusing nearly cost me my life. I had no choice but to take Hope and run."

The last bit of her story had apparently captured Hope's attention, as she looked up from her plate and placed her fork down. All joy had slipped from her face and a small pout now contorted her mouth. No doubt she was remembering that horrible night. Soleil wished she could erase it from the little girl's mind.

No one made a sound as they waited for Soleil to continue. She could feel the anticipation in the air, but had no plans to quell it.

Unable to hold back her curiosity, Virginia broke the silence. " нe Emancipation Proclamation was signed in 1863. нe 13th Amendment was placed into law two years ago. Why did you stay if you were treated in such a way?"

"Because freedom isn't free," Soleil snapped. She immediately felt guilty for the terse reply; Virginia was only trying to understand her situation, but Soleil's old rage over the plight of her people erupted from the depths of her heart.

"I beg your pardon? I don't understand."

"Not soon after the 13th Amendment came the Black Codes. If a Negro person is found without a job, they are charged with vagrancy. Vagrancy equals fines that you cannot pay. Not being able to pay equals imprisonment. But of course, no one will hire you without a reference from your most recent *employer*. For the Negro person in America, freedom comes at a cost most are unable to pay. Thus we are free on paper, but not free in fact."

Alex reached out and placed his hand atop hers. Soleil knew it was a gesture of reassurance, which was the only reason she did not follow through on her natural inclination to pull away. He had done so much, and was apparently feeling some guilt over her situation, so she would allow him this small measure of relief.

Before she knew what was happening, Soleil found herself once again encased in Virginia's solid embrace. Sobs racked the woman's body as tears ran down her face. For a moment, old habits of self-preservation kicked in, and Soleil went completely still. She reminded herself that the woman posed no threat, especially in her current, very round state, and relaxed into the embrace. Even surprising herself, she wrapped her arms around her friend to console her. Friend. It was a new concept, but one she could see herself getting used to. No one had ever cried on her behalf before. A small part of her melted at the thought, and yearned for more.

"Do not cry for me. That is simply the hand life has dealt me."

"Of course I am crying for you. I love you like my own flesh and blood. When you suffer, I suffer."

Soleil was momentarily taken aback by her words. She could feel the moment when the ice around her heart caved and Virginia pushed her way in. "I can never express to you how much those words mean to me. They touch my very soul. I am honored that you think so highly of me, but I still would not change a single minute of my life. Everything that has happened has brought me to this moment. It brought me my daughter, who is my greatest treasure, and the ability to feel your words and their importance with an appreciation I don't think many can fathom."

Soleil pushed out of the embrace to look Virginia in the eyes. She smiled at her and wiped away the tears. As she looked around the table, each face wore a similar somber expression. Hope looked as if she would disintegrate into tears if one more sad word was spoken. It was not her intent to make everyone so sad about her story.

"Stop your crying. We will blame it on the emotional turmoil the little one is stirring in you, and save my story for another day. In fact, if you wish and if Alex will allow it, I would love for you to call on me tomorrow."

"Of course I shall allow it. Besides, I have never been able to keep Virginia from barging into my home when the mood strikes her." Alex smiled and winked at Virginia with brotherly affection.

"I have no idea what you are talking about, Alex. I am a mild-mannered woman who only cares about societal decorum. I would never intrude on you uninvited."

"We will all ignore the lie of that statement," Charles interjected.

"What a treacherous husband you are! I will ignore that slight because I am such a gracious wife. And yes Soleil, I would love to visit with you tomorrow."

"Good, it is settled. Now it seems there is much I have missed in the past six years. Tell me the story of you and Charles."

Virginia's disposition brightened at the prospect of being able to share her and Charles's tale. "It is a most epic tale, if I do say so myself. Love, lies, danger, and adventure. Let's see, where to begin?"

Soleil relaxed into her chair to listen to her friend's recounting of what she would soon find was quite the epic tale indeed. Virginia had each of them hanging on her every word. Hope listened intently, as if she was afraid even to blink for fear of missing a piece of the story. The room was filled with love, laughter, and joy. It felt so strange and yet normal to Soleil. Taking it all in, she realized that normal was exactly what she needed.

Chapter Six

SOLEIL UNRAVELED THE FINAL braid from Hope's hair. They sat on the bed, the little girl happily playing with Mr. Snow. Despite the many dolls Alex had purchased for her, Mr. Snow was still her favorite. He was comfort. He had seen her through her hardest days.

Soleil kissed the top of her head. "All finished. It is time to sleep now."

"Yes, Maman." Hope crawled to the top of the bed and rested her head on the pillows, clutching Mr. Snow to her chest. As Soleil pulled back the covers to place over her, Hope turned to face her. "Maman, is Alex my papa?"

Soleil stilled. Her heart fluttered in her chest. It had been a long time since Hope had asked about the identity of her father. "Why do you ask that, mon amour?"

"You said my papa would be nice to me. Alex is very nice to me."

"That's very true, my love. He has been very kind to us both."

"Then he's my papa?" Hope's eyes overflowed with the desire for it to be true, and Soleil hated having to disappoint the little girl.

"You will know your papa when you find him. Your heart will be filled with love to the point you think it might burst. And he will love you just as much. You will never want to leave his side because he is a truly great man. *Comprenez vous*?"

"*Oui*, Maman."

Soleil bent to kiss Hope's forehead. "Go to sleep, mon amour. We can talk about this more another time."

Hope obeyed her mother's command and rolled on her side, closing her eyes. Soleil had known the day would come when Hope would ask about her father. She just wished that one day she would have a better answer to give.

Soleil looked down at the small girl with unending love. She brushed the hair back from Hope's face and kissed her one last time before drifing off to sleep.

"Tell me the reasoning again," Soleil said between giggles.

"Of course we had to save the kitten," Virginia explained, "even if it scratched and left us a bloody mess. We made a pact to be the protectors of all animals, no matter if they wanted the protection or not. How could we leave that poor kitten so high in the tree?"

"Yes, but self-preservation should have made us throw the ungrateful beast from the tree. I hear they always land on their feet anyway. Oh, the virtuous hearts of naive young ladies."

Soleil picked up the kettle to refill their tea cups. It was such fun sitting and hearing Virginia tell the many stories from their youthful adventures. Some even left her wondering if her brain had been fully functioning at the time.

"So tell me, how has it been, being reunited with Alex?" Virginia asked, wiggling her eyebrows suggestively. "We are both of age now. You can tell me all. Not that age would ever have stopped us."

Soleil nearly choked on her tea at the blunt and rather inappropriate question. She had a mind not to answer it, but with Virginia staring at her in eager anticipation, she didn't want to disappoint. Sharing the juicy tidbits of their lives was what friends did, she reminded herself.

Still uncomfortable, she fixed her eyes on the amber liquid in her cup. "I admit, I feel like my body remembers something my mind does not. It leaves my nerves a little frayed at times. Despite what my mind tells me, I cannot deny that I am attracted to him. In fact, my attraction seems to be growing each day, but I don't want it to."

Virginia sobered and placed her hand on Soleil's. "He would never hurt you. Alex has loved you for a very long time. In fact, losing you almost destroyed him."

"He mentioned something similar. It would be wonderful to believe in that, but it can never be. It's as if he lives in the sky, and I underground."

"Then we must teach you to fly. Alex is your epic tale of love. Do not miss it for any reason."

Soleil placed her tea aside and gathered Virginia into her arms. With a friend such as her, how could Soleil not be filled with optimism? "This visit has been a soothing balm on my soul. I was very lucky to have you as a friend in my youth, and equally lucky today. I would like to visit your home soon, if you do not mind."

"Of course! My door will always be open to you. We live no more than five miles away, just past the mill. We can visit each other often."

"Thank you. Now, tell me again the story of our egg battle," Soleil said as both women erupted into a fit of laughs.

Soleil was so happy she nearly skipped down the hall. Last night's dinner and her visit with Virginia this afternoon were the greatest times she could remember in...well, ever. She wanted to repay Alex for his continued kindness. Despite how much her brain told her she should not trust him, something in her wanted nothing more than to release the burden of doubt from her shoulders. Virginia's words of encouragement gave her faith that maybe she could.

She had decided to search out Vivian, because despite Alex's refusal to allow her to work in his home, she wanted to help around the house and show her gratitude.

She found Vivian in the sitting room, dusting the mantel. Not wanting to startle her, Soleil cleared her throat to get Vivian's attention.

"What do you want?"

From the beginning, Soleil could feel that Vivian did not like her, but she was filled with so much joy that the edge to Vivian's tone did not bother her.

"I wanted to see if I could be of assistance to you. Alex has been so gracious in letting me and Hope stay that I wanted to show my gratitude by helping with the upkeep of the house."

At first it looked as if Vivian would refuse her assistance, but Soleil could almost see the gears shifting in her mind. A twisted joy shone through her eyes, mirrored by her wicked grin. "As a matter of fact, I could use some assistance. You can finish the dusting and tidying up in here. I expect everything to be spotless."

"Not a problem, madam. It will be my pleasure."

Despite the venom with which the chores were given to her, Soleil was glad to be able to help. She took the duster and cleaning cloths from Vivian and immediately began to execute her tasks.

Vivian stood back, scrutinizing Soleil's work. Satisfied with Soleil's ability to complete the simple task of dusting, Vivian left the room.

Half an hour later, Soleil was finishing her job as she hummed the melody of an old hymn she had learned a few years back. It always soothed her and lifted her mood. A knock sounded on the front door, catching her attention. She could hear Vivian open the door and speak excitedly to the guest. A few moments later they entered the sitting room, and Soleil rose from her crouch. The guest was a petite woman with silky blonde curls fixed atop her head. She was the epitome of a southern debutant.

"You wait right here while I go get him for you," Vivian said before walking back out of the room.

The woman nodded as Vivian turned to leave. Just as she was about to pass through the door, Vivian turned back to Soleil and sneered, "Make sure not to miss a single speck of dust on any piece of furniture."

Soleil had the feeling the comment was meant to belittle her in front of the guest. At the sound of the snicker from the other woman, Soleil blushed in embarrassment. "*Oui*, madam."

Satisfied that her remark had caused its intended damage, Vivian turned again to leave.

Soleil noticed the smile slip from Elizabeth's lips the second Vivian had disappeared from the room. She shifted her gaze to Soleil, who dusted a nearby chest. Soleil could feel Elizabeth's heated glare on her back. She said nothing and continued her chores, staying aware of the woman behind her.

Slowly Elizabeth rose from her seat and sauntered toward Soleil. She stopped a few feet away and continued scowling at her. "Well, you are a pretty one. For a Negro woman, that is. I can see why he would find you appealing."

Soleil made no response to Elizabeth's taunt.

"But you do know he will never marry you."

"I do not know of what you speak."

"Do not play coy with me. Vivian told me all about how you two used to be inseparable when you were younger. How you looked at him with stars in your eyes. But I am the superior woman here, and I will have him in the end."

Soleil suddenly saw a flash of a younger Alex, teaching her how to aim a bow and arrow. They each laughed as she released the arrow and it flopped in front of her. For a moment reality mixed with memory, and the vision left her confused.

She shook her head to clear it and focus on the woman in front of her. "Ma'am, I do not know what claim you think you hold over Alex, but I am no threat to it. I honestly do not remember my childhood."

"That's right, you are supposed to have amnesia. You don't fool me," Elizabeth said, closing the distance between them. "I know you Negroes are crafty liars. You're probably making the whole thing up so he will feel sorry for you. You're wasting your time because I will be his wife in the end."

Soleil turned to stare Elizabeth in the eyes, her disdain apparent in her glare. Having Elizabeth crowd her space was triggering her instinct to defend herself. She needed the woman to back away, and soon. "Your inability to keep Alexander's interest has nothing to do with me. Alex is a grown man and will choose to marry whomever he pleases. Now please remove yourself from my presence this instant."

Elizabeth's mouth hung open in utter disbelief. "I have never been spoken to in such a manner! You will pay for your remarks."

"I do not fear your threats. Now, I ask you for the final time to remove yourself from my presence."

Elizabeth backed away slowly, unfamiliar with how to handle such a situation. Pure rage and embarrassment had turned her face a bright shade of red.

Once Elizabeth had backed away, Soleil turned on her heels and stormed from the room. She knew she should not have reacted the way she had, but if she had to pay for what she said, the look of sheer indignation on Elizabeth's face would make it well worth the punishment.

Alex scanned the books page again, yet the words still did not register. His joyful thoughts made reading impossible. How had he become so blessed? Having Soleil back in his life was pure bliss. A knock sounded, right before Vivian walked through the library's door carrying a tray of food that smelled like heaven. She placed it on the table next to his chair and smiled at him.

A feeling of apprehension settled over him at the sight of her. It was odd, because Vivian had been like the mother he'd never had. To be leery of her visits did not sit well with him.

"Hello, Vivian. How may I assist you?"

"I brought you something to eat. You look as if you could use a rest from all your work."

"It looks wonderful. Thank you." Alex took a bite and closed his eyes to savor the taste of the steak melting on his tongue. "It is as delicious as it looks. Please tell Cook she did a wonderful job."

"I made it myself," Vivian said, smiling at the compliment. "You are like a son to me and I am tired of this rift between us. I want to put it behind us."

Vivian took his free hand in hers and squeezed it reassuringly.

"As do I. I know you do not agree with all of my choices but thank you for seeking peace between us.

"I only want what is best for you, you know that. As my first act toward mending our relationship I have a surprise for you downstairs."

Alex rubbed the bridge of his nose, wary of the surprise Vivian had waiting for him. "You know I am not one who enjoys surprises. Please tell me what awaits me downstairs."

"I invited Elizabeth over for a visit."

Alex let out a sigh. It was just like Vivian to meddle in his affairs. He had been so consumed with happiness due to Soleil's return that he had completely forgotten about Elizabeth. "Since you invited her without my permission, you can have the pleasure of telling her to leave."

"That would be rude. That is no way to treat a lady, especially one you have been courting."

"I would hardly call our sporadic meetings a courtship. I do not wish to see her."

"As you wish. I will tell her to leave."

Just as Vivian was leaving his office, Alex had a thought. What if Soleil had seen her? What would she think of Elizabeth coming to call on him? "Wait. Where is Elizabeth, and where is Soleil?"

"They are both in the sitting room. One cleaning it, of course." Vivian smirked at her crude joke.

Without responding, Alex rose from his desk and walked to the stairs. He would have to take care of the situation before Soleil developed the wrong impression.

When he entered the sitting room, he looked around for Soleil. She was nowhere in sight.

Vivian entered the room shortly after him and sat in the corner to act as their chaperone.

After a calming breath, Alex turned his attention to the little blonde perched on the sofa's edge. She seemed a bit vexed, but Alex wasn't concerned with why. He needed her to leave. "Hello, Elizabeth."

As if by magic, Elizabeth's face transformed into one of joy and she beamed at Alex as he made his way toward her. "Alex darling, it has been so long since you've called on me. I was so pleased to receive your invitation. Where have you been hiding?"

"I've been busy taking care of business."

"You are such a hard worker. That is one of the many qualities I like so much about you."

"I am simply trying to run my plantation to the best of my ability, and to support those who depend on me."

"Which is why you have been so successful. I hate to start our visit on this note, but before we continue I wanted to inform you of Soleil's rude behavior. For no apparent reason, she verbally attacked me and stormed out. She is in need of a strong lesson in manners."

Alex groaned on the inside. He had hoped the two women would never cross paths. He knew Elizabeth was lying, but thought it wise to placate her. "I will make sure to look into the matter as soon as possible."

"Good. Oh, before I forget. The seamstress is putting the finishing touches on my gown for the Edwards' gala. It will be a splendid time," she said, injecting an extra dose of cheerfulness into her voice. No doubt she could read the disinterest written all over his face.

Alex cursed in his mind as his mood plummeted another ten feet. He had nearly forgotten about the gala, and that he was escorting Elizabeth. Every year the Edwards threw their pretentious summer gala to show off the newest items they had acquired during their travels. He hated the stuffy atmosphere and the boring conversations, but all the elite families in Elba would be there, and he could never pass on an opportunity to strengthen old business connections and make new ones. "I'm sure you will be a vision, no matter what you wear."

"You are too kind. Shall we go for a walk in the gardens?"

"I am sorry to have to cut this visit short, but I really have a great deal of work to attend to."

"You don't have a moment to spare? I have come all this way to visit you."

"Again, I am sorry, but I have important things I need to attend to." One of which was making sure Soleil was not infuriated with him. Alex could only imagine what Elizabeth had said to her. How was he going to fix this? Soon he would have to have a serious conversation with Vivian about interfering in his affairs.

Before Elizabeth could object further, Alex turned and left the room.

"Well, that was absolutely disastrous," Elizabeth said as she paced the sitting room. "I can't lose Alex, especially not to her. I'm the one who deserves a high-class gentleman. She must be using some dark magic to control his mind. I heard about all the voodoo and things they do in Louisiana."

Vivian crossed to the open door and stuck her head into the hallway. She peered left and right to make sure no one was in earshot, then closed the door to give them privacy. "Calm yourself, girl. You will have Alex in the end. I love that boy as if he were my own flesh and blood. I would never allow him to throw away his legacy. I will protect him from anything, including himself."

Elizabeth ceased her pacing. "How do you plan to do that?"

Vivian reached into her pocket and pulled out a folded piece of paper. She held it out to Elizabeth, who eagerly took it.

Elizabeth opened it with such force she nearly ripped it down the middle. Her eyes scanned the words, then she locked gazes with Vivian. "Is this really possible?"

"Of course it is. Just follow these directions exactly as I have given them. Soleil will be gone, and Alex will no longer be distracted from his pursuit of you."

"What of his feelings for her? Won't he fight for her?"

"Of course not." Vivian looked at Elizabeth as if the statement was truly imbecilic. "The feelings he thinks he has are the remnants of a childish fantasy. To choose her would cost him everything. He would not throw away all his family has built just for her."

Elizabeth nodded as if finally seeing the wisdom of Vivian's statement. Vivian liked the girl well enough, but knew intelligence wasn't her strongest attribute. There were probably a dozen other girls who would be better matches for Alex, but she had been the first girl he had even noticed since Soleil's disappearance—no matter how fleeting that notice had been. She would use whatever—or whoever—she had to in order to help Alex, even the little twit in front of her.

Chapter Seven

WEEK HAD PASSED since Soleil's encounter with Elizabeth in the sitting room. She had purposely been avoiding Alex ever since. She kept herself busy helping Vivian and taking care of Hope. The jealousy and disappointment she had felt at the possibility of Alex marrying the other woman confirmed what she feared: if she fully let him into her heart, he would destroy her. He could make her truly love him, and when he left her it would break her heart.

She lay in her bed, staring at the wall as she let her mind wander. Soleil had retired to her bedroom over three hours ago, but had been unable to fall asleep. Her sleep had become more and more restless lately as she dreamed about the couple she assumed were her parents.

In her dreams, they would all three be standing together talking until suddenly the couple began to fade. She would call out to them, but they continued to fade away until they had completely disappeared, and she was left unable to conjure any image or thought of them. She would be wrenched from her dreams panting and crying uncontrollably.

It was almost unbearable to have the image of these people in her mind and not being able to recognize them. It was as if the ability to truly remember and know them was at the edge of her brain, teasing her.

She got out of bed and quietly exited the room. It being past midnight, Soleil assumed everyone else in the house would be asleep.

Soleil walked soundlessly through the house, using the wall to guide her through the darkness. She walked until she came to the big oak door of the library. It had been so long since she had had the opportunity to sit and read a good book. She pushed the door open, stopping for a second when it croaked in protest, then continued when the noise subsided. She walked around the room, running her fingers over the leather spines of the books she passed.

It was too dark to see, but she didn't feel the need to light a candle. Any book would be a welcomed retreat for her mind, no matter its contents. She finally chose the last book her fingers came upon and picked it up. At the back of the library, a window seat allowed the light of the full moon to illuminate the small area. Soleil took the book over to the seat and curled her legs under her before she began reading.

Alex had been working diligently in his office. It was well past midnight, and the rest of the house was enveloped by sleep. He had already changed the candles twice and would need to do so again. It had been taking him much longer to complete his work since Soleil had entered his home. He often could not concentrate, his thoughts drifting to those beautifully sad eyes. He wanted so much to erase the hurt and replace it with the warmth he knew had once resided there.

But he didn't mind the extended work hours. It gave him a valid reason to avoid his bed and the demons that greeted him there.

Every time his thoughts turned to her, he would chastise himself for being so weak. Soleil deserved a better man than he could ever be. He was no longer the young man she had known. He wasn't even a fraction of him. War had transformed Alex from an optimistic seeker of adventure and glory into a mentally broken man. Soleil deserved a man strong enough to tackle the world for her—including his own mind—and lay the sun at her feet. He was not that man.

It would be best if he sent her back to her parents in France, despite her protests. Even though he knew it would be the best thing he could do, he just couldn't bring himself to let her go.

He knew she was avoiding him, but he wanted her to love him again as she once had. He wanted to see her eyes light up again with unrestrained joy when he walked into the room. It was selfish of him to want such things, especially since he could never give her marriage and the life that she deserved, but his heart would not listen to reason.

As he sat in his office consumed with thoughts of her, he heard a door creaking somewhere in the house. He stood from his desk and walked out of his office. It was dark throughout the rest of the house, but he did not take a candle so as not to alert the possible intruder to his presence.

He walked toward where the noise had come from, and

stopped when he came upon the library. he door was slightly ajar, just enough for a small person to slip through. He passed through the opening, grateful the door did not make any noise as he pushed it a little wider.

Nothing could have prepared him for the scene he came upon. After scanning the room, his eyes rested on Soleil sitting in the window seat at the back of the library. She had tucked her legs beneath her and leaned her head against the glass. The light of the moon set her honey skin and curly hair aglow. She looked so ethereal, like a fairy or some other mythical creature that existed only in the pages of books.

He ambled over to her as if pulled by an invisible line. When she finally became aware of his presence, Alex watched as what could only be described as sheer terror gripped her.

Panic filled her eyes, her breath coming in uneven gasps. She cowered behind the book she held as if he would strike her. "*S'il vous plaît pas.* Please don't... I'm sorry. I didn't think anyone... Please don't hit me."

Alex stopped cold in his tracks, mystified, hurt and angry at her suggestion that he might be so cruel as to hit her without cause. He didn't know which emotion was more powerful at that moment. "Why would I hit you?"

Soleil pulled the book slowly from her face, but continued bracing herself for a beating. "I invaded your library without permission. I should not have taken such liberties. I'm sorry—I couldn't help myself."

Alex clenched his jaw, then relaxed when he realized his expression might be fueling her fear. "Why would you think that would raise my ire? I have told you before and I shall tell you once more that you are a guest in my home. You may explore whichever portions of my home and estate you wish. I would never lay a finger on you for any reason, especially not over anything so trivial."

Soleil seemed to fully relax, tears slipping down her face. "I'm sorry," she said as she wiped them away. Each one she removed was replaced by another. "I don't know why I am crying. I seem to be a bundle of raw emotions as of late."

Alex's heart nearly broke for her. He sat next to her and gathered her into his arms. She leaned into his chest and allowed herself to sob into his shirt.

When she finally cried her last few tears, Soleil lifted her head and turned in Alex's arms, showing him her back. She pulled on her nightgown's neckline, exposing her bare shoulders and the top of her of her back. Scars crisscrossed the exposed flesh. "When I first came to be with Mrs. Williams, she caught me in her room without permission. I was putting away the laundry I had done. She told me that I was never to enter her private quarters without her permission. I received ten lashes for that mistake."

Alex had never dreamed of committing violence against a woman, but he wished more than anything he could have met Mrs. Williams, to return the treatment she had bestowed upon Soleil.

He put his hands on Soleil's shoulders and turned her to face him. He looked her in the eyes as he said, "I promise you I will never lay a hand on you as long as you live. I would like nothing more than to protect you. I failed you once, and I will never do it again. I hope I can once again regain your confidence someday. It would give me no greater joy than for you to trust me without hesitation."

"I can tell you are a very good man, but I do not know if I will ever be able to fully trust you. You are the embodiment of everything I have feared these past six years. That is my truth, no matter how much I wish it wasn't."

"When I lost you, I felt as if my entire world was ending. I couldn't sleep, couldn't eat. I would wake up every night from a horrible nightmare, sweating and gasping for air. I could not stop the images of all the horrible things that may have happened to you from flooding my mind. It would appear my imaginings were not too far from the truth. And then I went to war and fought next to men who wanted to keep alive the institution that had stolen you away from me. I cannot describe the guilt and sorrow that has plagued my every waking moment for so many years. Finding out that you were so close, and still I never found you, nearly kills me. I want to spend every day from now until I die making it up to you. I want to spend every breath in my body making sure you are safe and well taken care of. I do not expect you to ever love me again. In fact, I am not a man worthy of such a gift. But I will love you for the rest of my life, and my soul will love you for the rest of eternity."

Soleil's eyes softened on hearing his declaration. Maybe he would be lucky enough to one day get her to believe in what he said. "What about the woman who came to visit you?"

"I have never felt anything more than polite tolerance for Elizabeth. You are the only woman who fills my heart, the only woman whose beauty captivates me so fully that I wish I possessed the ability to write Shakespearean sonnets."

Self-preservation, trust, hope, fear. It was as if her thoughts were so palpable Alex could reach out and touch them. Her emotions warred across her face before she came to a final decision. With a deep breath, she said, "I admit I feel a connection and attraction to you as well."

A wide grin spread across Alex's face. He turned her again and pressed her back to his chest. He wrapped his arms around her, hugging her securely to him. "Good. Now tell me about your life for the last six years, and I will tell you about your life before then."

Soleil relaxed against him, and after a moment's pause began to tell her story. She told him about waking up in a wagon with no memory of who she was, or where she came from. How scared she was on the day she was sold. She told him about the good and the bad things that happened while working for Mrs. Williams.

"When I worked for Mrs. Williams, I did everything for her. I took care of her bills and all her accounts. I did her shopping and made sure she took her medicine. Every night I would read to her from whichever book she chose. That was my favorite part. I loved being able to get lost in the pages of a story."

"Where did you learn to handle money?"

"My father."

They were both struck momentarily mute from shock.

"How do you know that?"

"I don't know. The words just sprang from my mouth. Did I remember something?"

"It would appear so."

Soleil tried hard to remember something else. Anything else. "No other memories are coming to me."

"Don't force yourself. It is good that you have finally remembered something, and the rest will come to you in time."

"You are correct. It is frustrating having something in the back of my mind, but being unable to figure it out. We should change the conversation. Tell me about our past."

"As you wish."

Soleil released the need to have control over her memories so she could enjoy the experience of listening to Alex tell stories of the past. He told her about the many adventures they'd had together. Her favorite was about how he had learned to style her hair, which made complete sense because she still to this day loathed the task, and it was not a skill she could execute well.

They sat talking on the window seat for hours. Alex ran his fingers through her hair and gently stroked her arms. They lost track of the time, speaking with one another until the sun peeked over the horizon and shone through the window. Soleil had to get back to her room before Hope came bounding in from the nursery.

They both reluctantly rose and strolled toward the door.

"Thank you for sharing with me," Alex said.

"It was a great relief to be able to share the burden I have carried for the last few years, so I must thank you for caring and wanting to listen."

"It was my pleasure. I am willing to listen to anything you ever need to say. I want to spend more time with you."

"To what end? This night was wonderful. But we both know it cannot go beyond this."

"I love you with all that I am. No one will ever take that away from me. I will let nothing stand between us."

"You make such pretty declarations, but they cannot be more than empty promises. The law itself forbids our union. You cannot take on all of society. Perhaps we should cherish the memories from this night, and make it the first and last of its kind."

Alex didn't reply. Instead, he lifted his hand to graze his knuckles across her cheek. He lowered his head, his lips hovering above Soleil's in invitation. He wanted to kiss away all the doubt and hurt in her world, leaving only joy and hope for the future. Uncertainty swirled in the blue-green depths of her eyes, but Alex waited patiently. He wanted her to realize the power she had in this moment. The power she had over him at all times.

He could almost see the moment understanding dawned in her eyes. Even then she kept her distance. Right when he thought she would not accept his invitation, Soleil surprised him—and herself, based on her expression—by closing the distance between their lips. Her lips moved tentatively over his, exploring the sensation.

Alex wrapped his arms around her, pulling her in close. He wanted to keep the kiss gentle, but the desire that built in him with each stroke of her curious lips over his threatened that resolve. For a moment the kiss deepened, then he placed his hands on her shoulders and pushed himself back before his primal urges took over.

Soleil ran her fingers over her parted lips, her eyes never leaving his.

"Or maybe it can be the first of many more amazing nights to come," Alex said in a husky whisper. "Good night, my sunshine." Before she could respond, Alex turned her toward the door and gave her a soft push forward.

Soleil didn't protest as she walked through the door to return to her room.

Chapter Eight

*A*LEX COULDN'T CONTAIN HIS joy. The following evening could not have gone any better if he had imagined the perfect night in his head. He was so excited he no longer felt the need to sleep.

He had decided to use the extra energy to get some work done, but when he sat at his desk and looked over his schedule, he realized what day it was: April 24th. Soleil's birthday.

He immediately rose from his desk to plan what they would do that day. He made his way toward the nursery to retrieve Hope. Kneeling next to her bed, Alex smiled down at the sleeping girl. She was absolutely beautiful, just like her mother. Reaching out to gently rub her back, Alex tried to wake the sleeping child. "Hope, it is time to grace the world with your beautiful smile. Today is a very special day, and we have a very important assignment."

Hope stretched her little body before rolling over to face Alex. "Why is it special?"

"Because today is your mama's birthday."

Hope became fully alert, excitement filling her eyes. "It is?"

"Yes it is, and we are going to do something extra special for her."

"What? What?"

Alex chuckled at the little girl's enthusiasm. "Me, you, and Cook are going to make a meal for her, and then we shall take her on a picnic."

"Wow! That's fun. Let's tell Maman."

"We can't tell her yet. First, we must prepare the food. Then we shall tell her about the picnic. Can you keep it a surprise until then?"

Hope fervently nodded her head yes, her disheveled curls bouncing around her head.

Alex didn't think the smile on his face could grow any larger. He scooped Hope into his arms and headed toward the kitchen. When they arrived, Cook was already preparing dough for a loaf of bread.

"Good morning," Alex crooned. "I have a special request, if you would be so gracious as to grant it."

Amusement shone on Cook's face as she eyed them suspiciously. "That depends."

Alex put on his most charming smile. "Today is Soleil's birthday, and we would like to help you make her a delicious picnic."

"Last time you came near my kitchen you almost burnt it to the ground," Cook chastised, pointing her flour-covered finger in his direction.

"Really Cook, you need to learn to let go of the past. Besides, I was on my own then. Now I have you and Hope to help me."

"Yes, I will help!" Hope beamed.

"What will our assignments be?" Alex made a mock salute and stood at attention.

Hope followed his lead, standing tall, back straight, despite her broad grin ruining the effect.

Cook shook her head at their antics. "Little miss isn't even dressed. It ain't proper for a girl to be cooking in her night things."

"She is too young for 'proper' or 'improper.' Besides, it will save her dresses from getting dirty until we get her new ones. I think we can make an exception this one time."

"If you say so. Well in that case, little miss can help me with the bread, and you can chop the fruits and greens."

"Yes ma'am."

Alex and Hope followed Cook's instructions, but despite their best efforts, everything they helped with turned into a disaster. In the end, they watched and tasted while Cook finished preparing the meal. Once everything was finished and packed into the picnic basket, Alex carried Hope back up the stairs to Soleil's room.

Standing outside the door, Alex kneeled to Hope's level. "All right dear one, I need you to wake your maman. I would like the two of you to meet me outside at the wagon after the both of you are dressed."

Hope nodded before rushing through the door with excitement. What followed were the sounds of a very animated little girl shouting for her mother to wake up.

Alex went to get everything in order for their outing.

Soleil emerged from the front door, dragged along by Hope.

At the sound of their approach, Alex looked up from the horse he had been petting while patiently waiting for them to arrive. The smile that spread across his lips was enough to make any woman's heart stop.

Soleil couldn't help but smile back. She watched as he made his way around the wagon to assist them onto the bench. "Good morning, Soleil. Did you sleep well last night?"

"Good morning to you, too. I slept wonderfully. I hear we are going on a picnic today."

"Yes we are. I thought we could take a ride to my favorite place on the estate and stop to eat our meal."

"I helped make it, Maman!"

Soleil looked down at her daughter's proud expression and smiled. "Thank you both for being so thoughtful. I cannot wait to taste what you have prepared. What may I ask is the occasion for the picnic?"

"Your birthday."

Soleil's smile slipped. "My birthday?"

"Yes. Today, April 24th, is your birthday."

"How... how old am I?"

"You are two and twenty years of age."

Soleil became quiet, lost in thought. "Such a simple thing, yet I have wondered on it for so long. At least I now know." Soleil smiled at Alex and made her way to the steps of the wagon.

Alex helped her climb onto the seat, then squeezed her hand gently as a show of support. He could only imagine how hard it must have been on her not knowing even the simplest pieces of the puzzle that made up her past. Alex handed Hope up to Soleil, then made his way around to the driver's seat.

As they pulled off, Soleil closed her eyes and listened to the sounds around her. She allowed her body to sway with the gentle movements of the wagon. She hugged Hope to her side and reveled in the contentment that spread through her heart.

Yet again Alex had proven himself to be like none other. No one had ever cared to celebrate the day she was born, yet he was doing everything in his power to make her feel special. Despite how much she wanted to keep her heart at a distance, she could not help but feel gratitude and happiness that Alex had entered her life.

"You have such a beautiful estate," she said. "The scenery is so breathtaking."

"I am glad to see you still hold your love of nature."

"Nature is the one place where I can always find peace, no matter my circumstances."

"Yes, I remember. I specifically chose our destination with you in mind."

"And where would that be?"

"Look straight ahead, and you shall see."

Soleil looked in the direction Alex pointed. Not far into the distance she saw what appeared to be a garden. As they drew closer, Soleil's breath caught. It was the most beautiful sight she had ever seen. Ahead, a white fence housed a garden blooming with the lushest flowers in almost every color imaginable.

"Look, Maman! It's so pretty."

"You are right, dear one. The flowers are absolutely stunning." Soleil couldn't help but smile at the wonder on Hope's face.

"Can we pick some?"

"They are not my flowers. You will have to ask Mr. Cummings."

Hope shifted her expectant gaze from her mother to Alex. "Can we?"

"You can pick all the flowers you like."

"Thank you! Thank you!"

Alex chuckled at Hope's enthusiasm. A few moments later they arrived at the front gate of the garden. Alex descended from his seat, walking around the wagon to help the girls down.

As soon as her tiny feet touched the ground, Hope bolted toward the garden.

Soleil walked slowly next to Alex, stealing the occasional glance at his handsome face. He was such a gentleman towards her. Everything about her experience with Alex was new, and she loved every minute of it. As they entered the gate, they could see Hope already plucking flowers from the ground. Alex picked a spot for them to sit, spreading the blanket he had brought.

Soleil sat down, focusing on Alex as he pulled the food from the basket. "It strikes me as odd that a man of your standing would have such a garden."

"It was my mother's. She loved this place and worked in it herself. After her death, my father hired someone to maintain it in remembrance of her."

"I'm sure she would be very proud. Do you remember her?"

"No, she died giving birth to me. A fact I think my father blamed me for, although he never admitted it."

"I'm sorry to hear that. When did your father pass?"

"About two years ago. Him I do remember. I lived to please that man, but I was never good enough."

"Some nights I have dreams about a couple. I'm sure they are my parents, but I cannot be certain. I have learned the hard way the blessing of having your memories, which is why I strive so hard to remember every good moment in my life. I admit I have had more in recent weeks than in a long time."

Alex couldn't resist touching Soleil on seeing the gratitude radiating from her eyes. He leaned over and pulled her to his side. Soleil melted into the strength of Alex's arms.

Feeling her relax, Alex bent and kissed the top of her head. "You will regain your memory when the time is right. In the meantime, I promise to continue filling your days with many memories worth cherishing."

"Thank you for everything you have done. I can never thank you enough."

"When a man loves a woman, a thank you is never necessary. Knowing you are happy is more than enough."

Despite the sincerity in his words, Soleil could not bring herself to say the words Alex wanted and deserved to hear. "Alex...I—"

"I don't expect you to falsely declare your love just to please me. If the day ever comes when you can love me in return, I will be glad to hear you say it then."

"Why do you love me? Wouldn't it be easier to love someone else? Someone that you can proudly show in public. Our relationship can never be more than a secret."

"You are right, it would be easier to marry someone else. Someone with fair skin. But I fell in love with you. No matter what color you are, I will still love you and only you."

Soleil stared into Alex's eyes, searching for a hint of insincerity, but could find none. Could she really trust him to stand up for her against all others? It was easy to say such things when it was just the two of them, but only time would tell.

Just as she was about to speak, Hope came bounding toward them, breaking the tension of the moment. "Look, Maman. Look what I made."

Soleil focused on her daughter and the ring of flowers in her hand. "It is beautiful."

"It's a crown for you, Maman."

Soleil bent her head as Hope placed the flowers atop her crown.

"Doesn't Maman look pretty, Alex?"

"She most certainly does."

Heat bloomed on Soleil's cheeks at the compliment. To escape their previous conversation, Soleil quickly rose from the blanket, taking her daughter's hand. "Come, show me where you picked these flowers. I think I would like some more."

Soleil allowed Hope to drag her to every flower in the garden, and followed her daughter's order to sniff each one.

"Although pleasant, your presence is still a surprise. To what do I owe this lovely visit?" Soleil asked, walking into the sitting room.

Virginia rose from her seat on the armchair, pulling Soleil into a warm embrace. "I have come at Alex's request to take you and little Miss Hope on a shopping trip. He will pay the tab of course. I have been told to come home with no less than four dresses for each of you, and a complete wardrobe on order."

"I assume there is no way I can talk you out of this outing? I do not think Alex should spend his money on Hope and myself."

Virginia swatted her hand in the air, dismissing Soleil's comment as if it were the most ridiculous thing she had ever heard. "Of course he should! He has more than enough money to spare. Besides, he never spends it on anything enjoyable. I would like to think we are doing him a favor by enjoying his wealth for him."

Both women erupted into a fit of giggles.

"That may be, but I still don't know."

"Think of it this way: you are giving him the chance to store up good fortune by helping someone besides himself. You would like him to have good fortune, wouldn't you?"

"Of course," Soleil affirmed.

"Then it is settled. And I think the men wanted an excuse to have time alone. Manly bonding and all."

"Well when stated as such, how can I argue with you? I will collect Hope and we can be on our way."

Alex leaned across his desk, shoving Charles's crossed feet from its surface. "Thank the heavens you serve a purpose other than being a friend, because with your lack of respect for other people's property, who knows how long that would last between us."

"You couldn't live without me," Charles gloated, unaffected by Alex's statement. "I've taken the best care of you these past six years. Who else would brave the stench of your body odor to make sure you have engaging conversation?"

"My hygiene was only lacking for a brief stretch of time. My world had fallen apart. I had lost the woman I loved and survived a war that nearly tore this country apart. And it was my work that kept me sane—not your engaging conversation."

"You say work, I say my friendship. Let us agree that I am right and move on. What can I assist you with today?"

Alex ignored his friend's comment in lieu of getting down to business. "Yes, I need you to change my will. If anything should happen to me, I would like for Soleil and Hope to be taken care of."

"Of course. It is about time I use my law degree to help you do something good for someone else. I will draft up a new will in the morning. Anything else?"

"Yes, I..." Alex hesitated. Asking for help was not something he regularly did. "I need you to promise me something. I failed Soleil once, and I will never do so again. If I were to leave this earth before her, I need your promise that you will look after her."

Charles sat up in his chair, all seriousness. "Without question I will. She is not only the most important woman to you, but to Virginia as well. I promise you that as long as I live, she will be taken care of."

"Good," Alex breathed, relaxing into his chair. "Thank you, my friend."

"May I ask what your plan is while you are still among the living?"

"What do you mean?"

"You love her. I hope one day she will return the sentiment. What is your plan for when that happens? In the eyes of the law, she can never be your wife. Not in Alabama. And to parade around as such in the eyes of society would be dangerous."

"I would never risk her safety."

"So what will you do? Will you sell all you own and move to another state? One in which your union would be acceptable?"

"You know I can't do that." Alex crossed his arms, glaring across the desk at his friend. "This is my family home. I am a well-established member of this society, and my plantation depends on that. To leave would ruin me financially. Then I truly wouldn't be able to protect her."

"Being found to have a Negro wife would ruin you."

"No one will know if I do not tell them."

"And what of Soleil? Have you discussed this with her? Is she okay with you traipsing through society as if she doesn't exist? Does she know about the Edwards' gala?"

"No, I have not discussed it with her. And no, she does not know about it."

Charles shook his head. "In that case, my first tip for you on your road to marital bliss is that it is better to share too much rather than not enough."

"Why? It will only make her worry unnecessarily. I cannot tell her I will be attending the gala with Elizabeth. Not after their last meeting."

"As you wish, you arrogant bastard. Remember this moment when you are groveling for forgiveness. I pray she grants it to you." Charles rose from his chair. He bent deep at the waist with a flourish of his arm. "I think it is time I took my leave. Until next time."

Alex snorted at his friend's mocking gesture. At times Charles's imperious attitude grated on his patience. He needed practical advice, not fanciful, Utopian ideas. If the man didn't want to be helpful, the least he could do was keep his opinion to himself.

Dismissing Charles's words, Alex hardened his resolve to focus on protecting Soleil and figuring the rest out if—and when—the necessary time came.

Chapter Nine

*L*ADEN WITH BAGS, SOLEIL wondered if perhaps she and Virginia had gone a little overboard on their shopping trip. The coachman had made no complaints as he hauled her acquisitions into the house, but she had seen his strain under the weight of the packages. Hope had immediately wanted to show Miss Eliza her new dress, so she had escorted her to the older woman's cabin before returning to the house.

As she walked up the stairs to her room, she considered giving an account of her purchases to Alex. Soleil's thoughts were cut short as she entered her room and stopped mid-stride, taking in the sight that greeted her. Next to the window was an easel holding a blank canvas. Paints and brushes were arranged on a small table next to it. Attached to the canvas was a note written in bold, masculine print:

A very long time ago you stole my breath away with the most beautiful painting of a mountain landscape I have ever seen. I knew none before—and have known none since—who could match your talent and passion. It is my greatest wish to know that you have not lost that brilliant part of yourself.

~Yours truly,

Alex

With trembling hands, Soleil reached out to touch the brushes and paints. She felt the burn of tears as they collected in her eyes and ran down her face. Over the years, each time she had seen the painting supplies in the general store she had felt a pull toward them in her heart, as if they were calling to her. But such luxuries were the things of dreams.

Soleil chose a paintbrush, dipping it into the glass of water, savoring the weight and the feeling of rightness of it in her hand. She mixed a few of the pigments together, then dipped her brush in the paint. She dragged the brush across the canvas in one broad stroke. Then she stood back, staring at the single mark across the canvas, and the floodgates broke. Her body heated and trembled as emotions washed over her, almost to the point of being overwhelming. Sadness over what had been. Joy and hope for what could be.

Dipping the brush back in the paint, she made another stroke across the canvas. And then another. And another. Until her hand moved on its own, creating a picture her blurry eyes couldn't see. Blues, greens, and yellows splashed across the canvas. Her hand moved frantically to bring the image to life. She painted not with her conscious mind but with her soul.

She painted until the diminishing sunlight made it hard to see the canvas. Even then, her hand moved the brush until there it was: the image her heart wanted to paint.

The brush fell from her hands as she doubled over, sobs coursing through her body. Staring back at her from the canvas was the version of herself she wanted to be. Carefree and full of joy. Hope sat beside her with a brilliant smile. And like a shelter from the storms of life, Alex knelt with his arms around them. He was the epitome of strength and protection.

Soleil hugged herself tightly as she rocked back and forth on her heels in front of the painting. It was the thing she wanted most, and the thing that scared her the most.

Exhausted from the outpour of emotion, Soleil lay down on her bed and closed her eyes to rest.

She had come to the library because she couldn't sleep, and reading soothed her. That's what she told herself. But when Alex walked through the door as he did the previous night, Soleil knew that was a lie. Her heart rate quickened, and she had to fight to keep a smile from spreading across her face.

She said nothing as he crossed the room and sat next to her. To her surprise, he pulled a brush from his pocket and turned her so her back faced him. He pulled the ribbon from her hair and began brushing it from the bottom, working his way up. A feeling of home settled over her.

"Thank you for the paints and canvas. I can't tell you how much they mean to me."

"Have you used them yet?"

"Yes."

"What did you paint?"

Soleil ran her hand over her lap, smoothing out her nightgown. She picked at its fabric. "My heart."

"Will I be able to see it?"

Soleil could hear the double meaning in his question. "Maybe someday." She was glad her back faced Alex, so he could not peer into her eyes and see the truths they held. Steering the conversation to a safe topic, she asked, "Do you like running your plantation?"

Alex sat silently for a moment. "Sometimes I do, and sometimes I do not. It offers both a reprieve and a constant reminder of pain."

"I don't understand. How can it accomplish both things?"

"It offers me a reprieve from my nightmares. After the war, I began seeing the carnage and faces of my fellow soldiers who were not lucky enough to make it out alive. The plantation allowed me to throw myself into the work needed to run it, thus avoiding sleep and those demons."

"That's not good for your health. It will kill you."

"I know, but I would rather die than lose my mind. Besides, I have no family except a few cousins I barely know. No one would care if I were no longer among the living."

"I would care," Soleil whispered.

"That means the world to me." Alex kissed the top of her head.

"How does it bring you painful memories?" Soleil asked, uncomfortable with the emotional tension created by her statement.

"When I was a young boy about the age of six, I met a boy named Solomon. He was African, the son of one of my father's slaves. We began to play together during the day. We grew up together, and were best friends throughout our childhoods. When we were about fourteen, my father sold him. At that point we were like brothers, and it was like losing a part of me. When I begged my father not to sell him, he laughed in my face. He told me it was my fault for becoming attached to him, and that this was his business, and Solomon was his property to do with what he pleased."

"I am sorry for your loss. I have lost someone I felt was like a sister to me as well. I know that pain."

Alex was curious who she was talking about. Until this point, he had thought her life for the past six years was filled mostly with solitude. He found a little comfort in knowing she had had a friend at some point. "Who did you lose?"

"That is a long story for another night. But I promise I will tell you one day."

The death of her dear friend was something that Soleil had not spoken about with anyone, and she wasn't ready to do so yet. "I am reminded of her every day. The pain never really leaves you. How did you cope with your loss?"

"You helped me."

"How did I do that?"

"The loss of a brother had wounded me, causing me to be angry and bitter, especially toward my father. You helped me to be happy again. You helped me feel whole again. You surprised and amazed me with your simple wisdom and caring nature. It stunned me that your beauty on the outside matched what is within. Even though I knew my future would be one I despised, it seemed a little less daunting with you in it."

Soleil felt her heart flutter as she absorbed his praise.

Alex used his index finger to lift Soleil's face and kiss her tenderly on the lips.

"You surprise me as well," she said. "How could a man as kind as you have come to be in a world filled with such cruelty and hatred? But I am grateful for you all the same. Alex, I..." Soleil's words died on her lips as her mind screamed for her to keep them buried deep in her heart. But she needed to speak them, to give them life. "Alex, I love you, and it scares me to death. You have shown me more kindness than I have ever known. You see me not as an object, but as a person. But what can become of us? What can be our future? I wish to be no man's secret."

Alex kissed the top of her head. "I cannot tell you how much joy those words bring to my heart. Yes, you deserve nothing less than to be proudly displayed in society as my wife, but we both know that cannot be. But you will be the wife of my heart. I will cherish and protect you until the day I die. Can that, and my love, be enough?"

"Perhaps it can be. I do not know."

Alex scrubbed his hands across his face. "It is late. We will save these questions for another day. It is time for us to retire."

Soleil rose from the seat. "You are right, I am tired." She stood on her toes and kissed him on the cheek. While reason told her their union could never be, Soleil trusted in Alex. They would figure their situation out together.

❦

"I have a surprise for you."

Soleil's gaze shifted from the peas she shelled to Alex's handsome face. His jubilant expression was contagious, causing a hint of excitement to ripple through Soleil's body.

"Yet another? I am afraid at this rate you will spoil me into delusions of deserved grandeur."

"They shall not be delusions, my dear, for you deserve everything I can give to you and more."

Heat bloomed on Soleil's cheeks. She looked away with a shaky smile. "What is this surprise you speak of?"

"Another picnic. This time, only you and I," Alex said, undeterred by Soleil's dismissal of his compliment.

"That sounds like fun."

"Good. Meet me in the stables in fifteen minutes." Alex retreated from the kitchen before Soleil could ask questions.

The bank of a beautiful lake came into view after about thirty minutes of riding. Alex and Soleil dismounted, and Alex tied the horses' reins to a nearby tree limb. Soleil looked around at the beautiful scenery as Alex retrieved the food and blanket.

"What is this place?" Soleil asked.

The blue water reflected the sun, causing it to sparkle like diamonds. Soleil's gaze skimmed across the clear water. She noticed a small boat tethered to a pole on the shore, not too far from where they were.

"This was my favorite place to come as a child."

"Did you bring me here before?"

"Yes, I did. Many times, when you came to visit. We would lie in that boat staring up at the sky daydreaming for hours."

"That sounds lovely."

"This was the place I would escape to whenever I wanted to feel close to you when you were gone."

Soleil could see the happiness from the memories and sadness from the lost possibilities play across his face.

"Come. Please sit."

Alex laid out the blanket and sat on top of it with the food spread out before him. Soleil walked over to the blanket and sat next to him. Alex wrapped an arm around Soleil's waist and pulled her between his legs so that her back rested against his chest. She did not protest the embrace and closed her eyes as she laid her head against his shoulder.

Alex kissed her cheek and spoke in a low voice, "I have never brought anyone here. Everyone should have a place they find sacred and this is mine. I decided to bring you here to show you how much you mean to me. Only you have seen this part of my soul."

Soleil could think of nothing to say to such a declaration. He was bearing himself to her, heart, and soul. Instead of speaking she turned and kissed him with all the tenderness she possessed. As they pulled apart she said, "Thank you for sharing this with me."

"Thank you for understanding," Alex said with a tender gaze, as he rubbed his knuckles over her cheek. "Are you hungry?"

Soleil had been so busy dealing with Hope- who wanted to be particularly disagreeable this morning- that she didn't get a chance to eat breakfast before beginning her chores. She was ravenous and was glad that her stomach hadn't already announced that fact.

"Yes. Very, actually."

Alex picked up a bunch of grapes and pulled one from the stem.

"Open your mouth."

Soleil obeyed the request enjoying the intimacy of the gesture, even though it was silly because she was perfectly capable of feeding herself. When Alex brought the next grape to her lips Soleil playfully nipped at his fingers. Her breath hitched as desire darkened his intense blue eyes. As quickly as the desire appeared it was gone, replaced by a light-hearted gaze. Alex picked up a few grapes and placed them in Soleil's hand.

"Here take these and move back some. I want you to throw them at me and I will catch them."

"As you wish." She took the grapes and moved out of Alex's arms across the blanket. "Here they come."

Soleil threw the first grape and her eyes went wide with awe as she watched Alex dive over the blanket catching it in his mouth. Laughter flared in the depths of her chest and burst forth unbridled. She laughed so hard she had to hold her stomach to suppress the ache in muscles she hadn't engaged in a long time.

Alex swallowed the grape and said, "I thought you might find that amusing."

Soleil's laughter quieted as she replied, "How could one not find a grown man behaving in such a manner humorous? You looked absolutely absurd."

"A lesser man would be wounded by your statement. Since I am no such man, we shall do another. This time we will stand."

They stood, and one by one Soleil tossed the remaining grapes for Alex to catch. She continued to laugh at each jump, dive, or other maneuver Alex made to catch the grapes. She had almost forgotten how much fun something so simple could be. It was wonderful to be here laughing with him. When all the grapes were gone they sat back down to eat the rest of the fruit, cheese, and bread. Alex lay on his side in front of Soleil who sat upright looking down at him.

"Thank you, Alex. Thank you for giving me such a wonderful day."

"This is just one of many to come."

Soleil picked up an apple and took a bite as a distraction while she thought of a way to steer the conversation back to the safe, cheerful ground they had been treading.

"Tell me what your dreams for the future were when you were a boy. Adventurer? Philosopher?"

"Adventurer of course, like any proper boy. I wanted stories to be written about my journeys. And then a painter, a lawyer, a doctor, and anything else that didn't lead to my eventual fate of taking over my father's business. Then of course when I became a young man I wanted to be a loving husband to an extraordinary woman and father to the beautiful children we would be blessed with." Alex paused looking purposefully at Soleil. "At this moment I am beginning to think the last part can become my reality."

"Except that I can never be your wife. So alas, I think it will continue to be yet a dream."

A sly grin stretched across Alex's lips as if he knew something she did not.

"The great thing about dreams is that they belong to us so that we can shift and shape them to our liking. To make them fit with our reality."

"One can only do that with his own dreams and not with those of others. My dream is only for Hope's safety. I will do nothing to risk that. Since my dream is in opposition to yours I fear we are at an impasse."

"Your dream of Hope's safety is far from opposing my own. I would never see a single hair on her head harmed. Maybe one day I will figure out a way to make the rest of our two dreams one. I love a good challenge."

Alex's confidence was borderline arrogance, but it was a part of his strength that Soleil loved.

"Come let us go out on the water. I believe my old boat is still sturdy enough for two."

Alex rose from the blanket and extended his hand to help Soleil rise. She walked beside him to the little boat. Doubt and thoughts of potential disaster flooded her mind as they drew nearer to it. It had seen better days and it appeared dry rot had taken over a few of the boards.

"Are you sure that it can carry us both? It looks frail enough to break under the weight of a child."

Alex chuckled at her apprehension as they took the last steps toward the boat. He took hold of it and pounded on the side to test its stability.

"Yes, it is a bit older, but I know it will be strong enough for the both of us. Come, take off your shoes."

Soleil watched as Alex took off his boots and tossed them toward the blanket before doing the same herself. He rolled up the cuff of his pants then came and scooped Soleil into his arms. He waded into the water and deposited her in the boat.

"See, you are sitting in it and it hasn't broken yet. I'm sure you weigh more than a child, do you not." Soleil laughed at his quip. "It holds for the moment but let us see how it fares with your added weight. I'm sure that's equivalent to five or six children."

Soleil enjoyed their banter and the smile that seemed to be a permanent fixture upon her face whenever in Alex's presence.

Alex untied the boat and pushed it out onto the water. When far enough from the shore, he climbed into the boat and grabbed the paddle from beneath the seat.

"I am rowing us farther out onto the water and still we are safe."

"Next time I would still prefer a different boat."

"Next time you say. You give me hope that we will share a companionable outing again in the future."

"I am sorry to give you false hope. It was merely a slip of the tongue."

The smile slipped from Alex's face. Soleil swallowed, afraid she had gone too far and offended him.

"May I make a request of you? Ask a favor?"

"You may ask anything you like," Soleil replied earnestly.

"I admit I do not have a plan for our future yet, and I know you deserve more than I can give you. But I would selfishly ask that you do not fight our love. Instead, cherish it. If today were the last day we each had on this earth I want us to leave at peace, knowing that not even our greatest fears kept us from grabbing hold of the gift of our love."

Soleil rubbed her hands up and down her skirt as she sat in silent contemplation. Her mind screamed for her to resist the temptation in his words and protect herself from the pain that would inevitably follow. But her heart wanted nothing more than to enjoy every waking moment she had with Alex. Her pulse quickened, and nervous energy coursed through her veins as she pondered her choices.

"You make an excellent point and although I still find it a bit foolish I will agree with your request."

Alex let out a shout of victory. He placed the paddle back under his seat and pulled Soleil onto his lap causing the boat to tilt under the concentrated weight.

"You will not regret this. I will make you the happiest woman that ever lived." He brought his lips down to kiss her with the promise of what was to come. As they pulled apart Alex lifted Soleil in his arms and stood, rocking the tiny boat.

"*Attendre!* Wait!" Soleil protested.

Without heeding her objection Alex jumped over the side of the boat into the lake. They surfaced laughing while Alex held Soleil securely in his arms. Soleil pushed away and splashed water on his face.

"It was not my wish to get wet today."

"I was attempting to be thoughtful. You looked as if you could use relief from the heat." Alex replied with a playful grin.

Alex swam towards Soleil only for her to swim away. When he no longer pursued her, she laid back floating across the water looking up at the sky.

"A great relief it is. But now my clothes are soaked through. How will it look if we return dripping wet?"

"True. We should return to the shore to dry in the sun."

They swam back to the boat and climbed in over the edge. Alex took hold of the oars and began directing them back to the shore. Once back on land they laid on the blanket and Alex pulled Soleil to his chest and gently stroked her hair.

"Thank you for today. I believe I needed it more than I realized."

"As did I. You are most welcome."

Soleil replayed the day in her mind and enjoyed the feel of Alex next to her. After a while, she heard his breathing deepen and looked to see him asleep beside her. She closed her eyes and joined him in sleep.

Chapter Ten

ALEX HUMMED TO HIMSELF as he worked. In his mind's eye, sonnets depicting the greatest loves merged with images of Soleil. She had brought to life a part of him he had long since thought dead. Even laboring in the field, planting corn under the harsh sun didn't dampen his mood. Many of the men enjoyed a good laugh at his expense due to his excessive cheer.

"Mr. Alex! Mr. Alex!"

Alex wiped the sweat from his brow with his forearm as he looked up to see a frantic Joseph sprinting across the field toward him.

"Mr. Alex! Mr. Alex!"

"Yes, Joseph? What is it? And slow down, boy. You look like you are going to topple forward any minute."

"Come quick, Mr. Alex," Joseph said, coming to a halt in front of Alex. He barely took a breath before he grabbed Alex's arm and tugged him toward the house.

"Hold on now. What's the matter?"

Joseph stopped to stare at Alex, as if his question was a waste of precious energy and time. "The sheriff showed up saying he's gonna take Miss Hope. Says he has to return her to her rightful caretaker, Mr. Williams."

"What? And he is here now?"

"Yes, sir."

Alex's heart slammed against his rib cage. "I'll handle this." This had to be a mistake. James had no claim to Hope. How could he possibly attempt to steal her away?

Alex pushed his legs to run as fast as they could carry him. He needed to find Soleil before he handled the situation with the sheriff. He could only imagine the fear and worry she must be feeling. Hope was her entire world, and any threat to her would crush Soleil.

Alex bounded up the back porch steps into the kitchen. His anxiety heightened when he didn't find Cook in her normal spot, stirring the pots in preparation for one of her delicious meals. In fact, hardly any noise greeted him. No cleaning, no talking, no laughing.

"Soleil! Hope! Where are you?" As he left the kitchen and entered the hall, running toward the stairs, Vivian emerged from the sitting room.

"Alex! Please come. The sheriff wishes to speak with you."

Did his eyes deceive him, or was Vivian pleased to deliver that bit of information? At the moment it didn't matter, he reminded himself. "I need to find Soleil first. She must be out of her mind with fright."

"She is in her room. I think it best if you talk with the sheriff first. You might be able to defuse the situation if you talk with him."

Alex looked up the stairs, then toward the sitting room. There was wisdom in Vivian's advice. Maybe it would be better if he handled the sheriff first. Then he could comfort Soleil with the news that the situation had been handled.

Head high, he strode into the sitting room and glared down at the portly older man lounging on the sofa. The sheriff was generally a decent man, and Alex had never seen him as an enemy. But as the current source of Soleil's distress, Alex had about as much compassion for him as he would a rabid dog.

The sheriff stood, his motion unhurried, his voice relaxed as he stuck out his hand. "Good afternoon, Mr. Cummings. Thank you for seeing me."

Alex shook the offered hand with a bit more force than necessary. "Sheriff. What can I do for you today?"

A slight wince vibrated through the sheriff's body at the contact, but to his credit, his hard gaze never left Alex's.

"I've come to collect the girl, Hope. Her owner said she was taken without his permission. He wants her returned."

"As a man of the law, you should know that slavery is no longer an institution that exists. As such, Hope has no owner. She will not be leaving with you today—or any day, for that matter."

"She may be free, but Mr. Williams still has rights to her. This is something I learned, being a man of the law and all," he said, relishing his perceived upper hand.

"And what rights would those be? Never mind, this conversation is over. Hope is not here right now, even if I had lost my mind and thought of handing her over to you."

"Is that so?" he said, tilting his head, eyes narrowed on Alex. "Shame. Mr. Williams will be disappointed. I guess I will have to come back tomorrow."

"You do that."

"Listen, son," he said, leaning in like a sage about to impart wisdom to a young apprentice, "I heard the rumors about you in your youth. How you were head over heels for some young Negress. And this Hope is her daughter. Normally I don't much care what a man does in his own home, but you can't air your dirty laundry to the world. Don't make this more than it needs to be. You will lose everything in the end."

"Is that a threat?" Alex asked between clenched teeth.

"Nope. Just a fact," he said with an easy grin. "You have a good day now."

The sheriff sauntered past Alex, whistling an upbeat tune.

Soleil paced back and forth across her room, wringing, and shaking her hands to calm her frayed nerves. It felt as if a rock had taken up residence in her stomach. She chanted to herself that everything would be fine, but her heart wouldn't believe it, no matter how badly she wished it would.

Images of Hope being pried from her arms ran through her mind, making it hard to hold back the scream that wanted to explode from her chest. As she paced the room, the door crashed against the wall as Alex burst in.

Soleil rushed into his arms, pouring all her fears and doubts into his crushing embrace.

"Are you well?" Alex asked. "Where is Hope?"

"I sent her with Miss Eliza. We need to leave," Soleil urged, running her clammy palms over the skirt of her dress. "How could James take her? He has no claim to her."

"Calm yourself. All will be well in the end."

"How do you know? I can't lose Hope. I..." Soleil's voice broke on a sob. "I can't."

"And you won't. It is my duty to protect you, and I will never fail in that duty again. We will leave at once to talk with Charles. He can walk us through our legal options."

"And what if there are no legal options?"

"I said I would protect you, no matter the cost. I plan to honor that promise," Alex declared. "Prepare to leave at once. I will be waiting in the carriage."

Alex pulled her in for another reassuring embrace before kissing her forehead and leaving the room. As much as she wanted to believe him, Soleil's mind went to work formulating her own plan in case the legal option failed.

As Alex walked toward the front door to meet Soleil, he stopped when he saw Hope merrily skipping behind Miss Eliza. She held some food in her hand he could not identify, but was probably of the sweet variety.

As she chewed, she turned and saw him standing in the foyer. "Alex!"

Alex bent to his knees and opened his arms to capture the little girl as she ran to him. "Hello, little one. How are you on this fine afternoon?"

"Good. Ms. Eliza gave me chicken."

"Is that so?"

"Yes. Want some?" Hope shoved the half-mauled piece of meat in his face in offering.

"That is very kind of you, but I have already eaten."

"I'm saving some for Maman. She said I had to stay with Miss Eliza until she called for me."

"Is that so? Well, your maman and I are going into town today, so I will make sure she gets something to eat. You enjoy the rest of your chicken."

Hope's eyes beamed with the knowledge that she no longer had to share. Then her eyebrows crinkled as if a profound question had entered her mind, requiring deep thought. "Are you my papa?"

Alex's mouth hung open, caught off guard by the question. Of all the things that could have come from the little girl's mouth, this was the last he would have expected. "Do you think I am?"

"Maman said I would know my papa when I see him. That he would be a man who loved me and Maman. Do you love us?"

Alex's chest puffed in pride at the little girl's intelligence and boldness. "Yes, I love both you and your mother very dearly."

"Then you are my papa?"

"I would love nothing more than to be your papa."

Hope wrapped her little arms around his neck as she squealed with joy. "Papa, can we have Christmas?"

"Of course."

"Good, I never had Christmas before. For my present can I have a baby sister?"

Alex barked a booming peal of laughter. "We will have to discuss that with your maman."

"I will ask her."

Miss Eliza cleared her throat, reminding them she was listening. Her eyes twinkled with laughter.

"It would appear Miss Eliza is waiting on you, and your maman is waiting on me. We must go."

"All right, Papa. I love you."

"I love you, too." They exchanged one last hug before Hope and Miss Eliza continued on their way.

Alex strode through Charles's office door, finally able to repay him for all his uninvited intrusions. Soleil entered soon after.

Charles peered with mild interest over the top of the daily newspaper he had been reading. "To what do I owe this unexpected visit?" he asked with a smile for Soleil, ignoring Alex.

"We are in need of your legal counsel," Alex interjected. "The sheriff came to the house today, requesting we hand over Hope. He said James alleges that Hope was taken without his permission, and he wants her returned."

Charles came to attention, eyes hard. He folded the paper in an unconscious gesture, shoving it to the edge of his desk. "Did you give her over to the sheriff?"

"Of course not," Alex scoffed. "Slavery is over. He has no right to ask for her return. But he said he will return in the morning."

"I am sorry to be the bearer of bad news, but James might have a legal leg to stand on."

Soleil choked on her next breath as all color drained from her face, leaving it the ashen, tawny brown of a dying fawn. Alex reached out in time to catch her before her knees buckled. He held her trembling body close, rubbing his hand over her back in support.

"Explain," Alex barked.

"Last year the state legislature passed a series of laws restricting the rights of the newly freed. They have acquired the moniker 'The Black Codes.' One such law governs the relationship between a master and apprentice. It is a loophole, if you will, one of many, for former masters to keep the children of their former slaves. It allows the former owner to keep the children of their slaves if the slave is found unable to care for the child on their own. If the apprentice were to leave without their master's consent, he has the right to have the apprentice returned."

"Are you saying he will claim Hope as his apprentice?" Alex demanded.

"Yes, that is what I believe."

"How is that possible? I was the one who worked for him. Not Hope."

"Yes, but as you were the former slave of his mother, and then under his employ afterward, it could be argued that you were unable to care for Hope on your own, thus he took her on as his apprentice."

"That's not right! How can they do that?" Soleil shrieked.

"What are our options?" Alex asked, voice stony.

"Perhaps you and I should discuss the options in private. I fear the remainder of this conversation may not be suitable for Soleil to hear."

"No, please. I need to hear what can be done," Soleil begged.

Her pleading eyes twisted Alex's heart, making him unable to deny her anything. "Continue. You may speak freely in front of her."

Charles warily glanced between Soleil and Alex. "As you wish. You could claim Hope as your own."

"I don't follow. What do you mean? How will that help?"

"Soleil is five years old. She was born not long after Soleil was abducted. We can claim that Soleil was pregnant before she went missing, and that you are the father. This will make you Hope's rightful guardian."

"Could that work?"

"I believe it is our best option. But if we take that stance it may cost you everything, Alex. Your reputation will be ruined. I advise you to go home and think on it. I will get an injunction prohibiting the sheriff from removing Hope from your home until we go to court, if that is what you choose."

"Yes, get the injunction and I will be in touch soon with my final decision."

"Good. I have a friend who owes me a favor. There is a high chance I can get us on the docket as early as next week."

"Thank you."

Alex's stomach sank. The weight of the decision was like a crushing stone on his chest. Eyes wide and vacant, Soleil stood next to him, not making a sound. The only signs of life were the slight tremors coursing through her body.

Alex said a silent prayer for guidance on what to do next.

Alex and Soleil sat next to each other, each lost in their own thoughts, as the carriage ambled along its bumpy journey. Soleil stared out the window with the same blank expression she'd worn since leaving Charles's office.

Alex wanted nothing more than to gather her in his arms and tell her that all would be well in the end. "Soleil, you have nothing to fear. I will protect both you and Hope."

"No. You can't," she deadpanned.

"Of course I can, and I will."

"You can't," she repeated, finally meeting his gaze. "To claim Hope as your own would cause your business associates to shun you. Your plantation would not survive the blow. Too many people depend on you to let that happen. This decision isn't only about Hope—it's about all the families that rely on you to keep them fed and clothed. You can't do it, and I..."

The whistle of a train in the distance caught Soleil's attention, and her words died on her lips. She sat up straight in her seat as a plan flashed through her mind. "Stop the carriage," she shouted.

Alex blinked rapidly, caught off guard by Soleil's sudden outburst. After a moment's hesitation he followed her command and tapped the roof of the carriage, signaling the coachman to stop.

Soleil leaned forward and grabbed his hands in hers, a wide smile adorning her face. "I know what to do. When you first found me, you suggested I return to my family. I was hesitant then, but now it is the only way to save Hope. Will you honor that offer now and pay for our passage to France?"

Alex stared back at Soleil, lost for words. His heart constricted in his chest. She wanted to leave him. Losing her the first time nearly destroyed him. Doing so again would finish the job. But what choice did he have? She was right.

"As much as it pains me to do so, I will. I will have the driver take us to the train depot, and we can purchase tickets to New York. From there I will purchase passage for you and Hope to France."

Alex could see the moment the reality of her request dawned on Soleil. France was somewhere he could not follow her. Returning home meant losing him.

Chapter Eleven

OUR DAYS. SOLEIL STARED at the date on the ticket in her hand. In four days she would be boarding a train to New York. In four days she would begin the journey of leaving behind the man her heart begged for.

"Put that away," Virginia chided, pushing the offending document away from Soleil's line of sight.

Soleil obeyed, folding it into a small square before clutching it in her right fist. "Why must life be filled with so much pain? Why must I have to continue to sacrifice so much simply to survive? Will there ever be a day when I can thrive?" Soleil asked.

Virginia stroked her hair as Soleil rested her head in her lap. Tears spilled from Soleil's eyes, dampening Virginia's dress. "I know. It is not fair. You both deserve to be happy. You deserve each other."

"But that cannot be."

"Perhaps it can be. Allow Alex to claim Hope."

Soleil closed her eyes against the crushing heartache. It would be all too easy to give in to the temptation and do exactly that. To allow herself this one bit of happiness. She wanted to yell, scream, and rage against the unfairness of the situation, but if life had taught her nothing else, she knew that expecting fairness was as useful as trying to avoid droplets of water while standing in the ocean. "To do so would be an act of pure selfishness on my part. I cannot do such a thing to those who depend on him."

"We all deserve to be a little selfish on occasion," Virginia grumbled with a snort.

"Not like this. Besides, I still haven't told him yet."

"Goodness." Virginia's eyes went wide as she paused mid-stroke. "Why not?"

"I wanted to when Charles made his suggestion, but I didn't have the courage at the time."

"Yes well, there is no time like the present."

"I cannot handle more truth. Please stop."

"Never. I am your truest friend. As such, I speak truth whether you wish to hear it or not," Virginia reprimanded. Her tone softened. "But I think you have had enough for the moment. Lay here and rest a while. Then go home and tell Alex the truth."

"He will not be in this evening. He mentioned having business to attend to that would keep him out late."

Guilt flashed across Virginia's face. Soleil's brows furrowed in confusion. Perhaps she had imagined it. What did Virginia have to be guilty about? But her friend seemed to suddenly have a hard time meeting her gaze. "Yes well, tomorrow then."

"If I must."

"You must. I will take my leave now. The carriage will be ready to take you home after you rest."

Virginia rose from the bed, leaving Soleil alone with her thoughts. Dread settled over her. She was not ready to face this, but she must do what needed to be done.

⁘

The large front door of Alex's home opened, granting Soleil entry.

To her surprise, Vivian stood holding the door open with a genuine smile plastered to her face. "Good evening," Vivian trilled.

Soleil frowned at the warm greeting. "Good evening," she said before stepping past her into the foyer. Her steps faltered a few feet over the threshold. In the sitting room, Elizabeth sat perched on the edge of the loveseat, dressed for an evening out, and possibly more.

Her silky blonde hair was braided and curled in an intricate design fixed atop her head. She wore a stunning blue dress that complemented her eyes, turning them into glimmering sapphires. The front of the dress dipped low, almost to the point of being immodest, showing off full, milky white breasts. That dress was meant to entice and capture any man she set her sights upon.

Soleil looked down at her simple green dress. Alex had told her she looked radiant in it, but compared to the vixen sitting a few feet away, Soleil wondered if he would look twice at her now.

A soft chuckle sounded behind Soleil. A devilish grin greeted her when she turned her focus back to Vivian. She was relishing in the pain she caused Soleil. Neither woman spoke to Soleil as she stood frozen before them. Instead, heads held high, they each wore identical expressions of imperious superiority.

Without a word to either woman, Soleil ran to the stairs, headed to Alex's room. Her mind raced with so many questions. What was Elizabeth doing here? Why was she dressed for a ball? Lost in thought, Soleil nearly ran into Alex as she crested the landing of the second floor. His arms reached out in time to keep them from colliding.

The smile he greeted her with vanished as he looked into her narrowed eyes. "Has something upset you?"

"Why is she here?"

"To whom do you refer?"

"Now is not the time to be coy," Soleil accused. Her nostrils flared as a raging heat spread throughout her body.

Alex glanced around Soleil to the maid dusting a lamp a few feet away. "We should discuss this in private."

Alex placed his hand on Soleil's elbow and guided her to the library. He stopped at the room's entrance to allow her to precede him, but as soon as he entered and the door was closed, Soleil rounded on him, accusation dripping from every word she spoke.

"Why is she here?"

"Again, to whom are you referring?" Alex asked in a clipped tone. Annoyance laced his words, but Soleil didn't care. She had the right to be angry, not him.

"Elizabeth. Why is she downstairs?"

"Elizabeth?" Alex's words were cut short as understanding dawned on him. "Soleil, I am sorry. I should have told you."

"Then it's true. You intend to escort her a social function of some sort tonight?"

"Yes, but for a specific purpose."

"And what purpose would that be?" Soleil spat. She stepped out of his reach and crossed her arms over her chest as Alex attempted to grasp her hands.

Faced with her denial, Alex let his arms fall to his side. "Every year, Mr. and Mrs. Edwards hold a gala to celebrate their travels. I must go to make a good impression and converse with current and future business associates. Not going could offend and cause damage to some of my key relationships."

"You still have not explained her presence."

Alex ran his hands through his hair, then released a frustrated breath. "I agreed to escort her before you returned. Many in attendance are expecting us to arrive together. In the minds of some, we are practically engaged. I must make necessary appearances until the time is right."

"And when will that be?"

"I don't know," Alex growled, slamming the side of his fist into a nearby bookshelf. Soleil didn't flinch from his sudden outburst. No part of her felt any sympathy for him.

"The society gossips have already taken note of you being here, and what you meant to me in the past. The sheriff alluded to as much. I didn't want to give them any more fodder for their flaming lips. It could have led to a dangerous situation for you and Hope."

"Do not lay this at my feet!" Soleil shouted, slicing her hand through the air. "I will not be the excuse for your lies. You were thinking about yourself. Your reputation. I can't believe I trusted in you. Even if I had agreed, you would have never claimed Hope, would you? The cost is more than you are willing to pay."

"Soleil, please. I didn't want to hurt you."

"Like you're doing now?" Tears fell silently down her cheeks. "I almost feel sorry for you. You have lived in a world that catered to you your entire life. You have no idea what it means to sacrifice for those you love. Nothing in life is free, not even love. We must all pay a price, or leave this world only having experienced a fraction of its potential joy."

Alex visibly recoiled from the sting of her words. He rubbed the heel of his palm against his chest as if he had received an actual blow to the heart.

A new sadness fell over Soleil. Not for herself, but for all the love Alex would miss in his lifetime. Soleil wrapped her arms around herself, eyes cast down as she walked past Alex to the library's entrance.

Alex followed and caught her arm in his hand before she reached the threshold. He turned her to face him, but before he could speak the door opened as Vivian strode into the room.

"Please pardon the intrusion, but I heard a commotion as I came near the door. Is all well in here?"

Soleil pulled free from Alex's grasp. Her heart was filled with so much sadness, she didn't even feel a twinge of anger at the false mask of concern on Vivian's face. Instead, she was grateful for the distraction. Without another word she slipped from the room.

"Well, we can't leave your guest waiting, can we?" Vivian chirped.

Books went flying as Alex swept his arm across a shelf. Rounding on Vivian, Alex jabbed a finger in her face. "I told you that I would be picking Elizabeth up from her home," he seethed.

Vivian's mouth opened and closed as her eyes widened until Alex could see the whites. He had never directed this much fury at her before. "I... I... I thought..." she stammered. "I thought it would be a lovely surprise for her to come here. I didn't think you would mind."

"Well you thought wrong. Do not think for a second I do not see through you. I will deal with you when I return," he snapped. "Tell her I will be down momentarily."

Without another word, Vivian exited the library, shutting the door behind her.

Alex cursed himself for making such a mess of things. Soleil's words echoed through his mind. Would he have claimed Hope if she had allowed it? He wanted to think he would, but a part of him questioned if that were true.

Despite the myriad of emotions churning in his mind, Alex reminded himself that he had other pressing matters to attend to. After he concluded his appearance at the gala, he would handle the situation between himself and Soleil. Alex took one last calming breath, then headed down to greet his guest.

Alex sat in the carriage across from Elizabeth, staring out the window. He made for a lousy companion with the scowl marring his face and his inability to concentrate on a conversation. But Elizabeth seemed not to notice as she chattered away, filling in his lulls in the conversation.

How he had left things with Soleil hung over his head. The urge to go home and beg for her forgiveness ate away at his desire to attend the party. "I'm sorry, but I am not feeling up to going tonight. We will return to my home, and I will have a carriage return you to yours."

Alex tapped on the roof of the carriage, then opened the window to instruct the driver to turn around.

"So you can be with that Negress of yours?" Elizabeth's stare bore into his.

"What did you say?" Alex went still as he assessed the woman across from him. Gone was the sweet wallflower he had known until this point. In her place was a vicious harpy, ready to attack her prey. Had her charming manner and gentle countenance caused him to underestimate her?

"You heard every word I spoke," she hissed.

"I know not of what you mean." Alex fisted his hands in his lap.

"Do not be obtuse. I have no room for games. Vivian told me everything. About how you and Soleil have loved each other since you were young." She drug out the syllables in the word "love," making it sound like an antiquated idea only children were naive enough to believe in. "I have no problems with your dalliances with Soleil. In fact, I am willing to make you a deal. I need a husband to keep me out of the poor house, and you need a wife to keep your reputation unchallenged while you take her as your bed wench. A marriage could be a mutually beneficial arrangement."

"I am sorry that you have been misinformed. I have no such concern or need for a wife of convenience."

"I am a patient woman, but do not test me." Elizabeth leaned forward with a look that radiated superiority. "Luckily for you, I am feeling generous this evening. I would like to add an additional incentive to the deal. Marry me, and your troubles with James will disappear."

Every muscle in Alex's body coiled with rage. Searing heat engulfed him. His teeth ground together, and his fists clenched and unclenched as he tried to calm himself enough to speak. "What part did you play in that?"

"What does it matter now? What is done is done. Will you accept my offer?"

"I will never marry you, and you will pay for your actions," he whispered with deadly calm.

Alex could see the flash of uncertainty in her eyes. She slouched back into her seat, a deflated version of her former arrogant self.

"Halt," Alex shouted as he punched the roof of the carriage several times. Before it had even come to a complete, stop Alex jumped from the small space. He instructed the driver to return Elizabeth home before starting the mile walk in the pitch-black back to his estate.

Chapter Twelve

OLEIL LAY ON HER bed, staring into the darkness. Her argument with Alex played through her mind on a constant loop. The more she reviewed the events, the more she understood his dilemma. In a perfect world, a man would choose a woman without hesitation or thoughts of the consequences. But this world was far from perfect. Each action and choice had consequences that rippled into the lives of others. She wanted no bitterness to reside between them. The need to apologize to Alex kept her eyes open, despite the late hour.

Heavy footsteps echoed outside her door. Her heart soared, ready for the chance to make amends with Alex. But when the door burst open to reveal Vivian, followed by a large man holding Hope, Soleil's heart fractured into tiny pieces. Tears spilled down Hope's face into the rough hand covering her mouth.

Soleil jumped from her bed, staring between Vivian and the large man. "What are you doing with my daughter? Unhand her this instant."

Vivian ignored her statement as if it were a waste of breath to even acknowledge her existence. "That one," she said, pointing to Soleil. The man advanced toward Soleil and plucked her off the bed as if she weighed nothing.

Soleil kicked and clawed at the man, but attacking a brick wall would have been a better use of her energy. He flung her over his shoulder and waited for the next order.

"Calm yourself, wench," Vivian bellowed.

Soleil stilled and looked at her. "Why are you doing this? Alex will..."

Vivian slapped her across the face, cutting off her words.

"Alex will never know. I will tell Alex that after your heated argument, you decided to leave immediately and try to find your own way home. I thought having James take Hope would be enough, but now I see the error of my ways. You can't just leave—you need to be destroyed. Alex will always hold you in his heart while you are alive. I will not see Alex fall to ruin over a Negress. You are not worthy of being the dirt beneath his boots."

"Please take me, but leave Hope alone."

"You can't possibly think I would do such a thing. Don't waste your breath begging. I've found a lovely home for her in an upscale brothel," Vivian gloated with a sinister laugh.

"No!" Soleil wailed. She resumed kicking and beating against the man's strong hold. As before, her efforts had little effect.

"Take her away," Vivian commanded.

Joseph crept to the edge of Soleil's door. He had seen when the large man had ridden up, and upon seeing him talking with Vivian, decided to follow them. The conversation reached his ears from the open door. Vivian's harsh words about destroying Soleil crashed into his heart.

Mr. Cummings would be devastated if anything happened to Soleil, especially under his own roof. Besides that, she was one of the kindest women he knew. She always had an encouraging word or smile for him. She didn't deserve the fate Miss Vivian had planned for her.

Joseph knew he needed to act soon, but didn't know what to do. It would be impossible for him to face the large man alone. He needed help. Miss Eliza. She would know what to do.

Joseph crept back to the stairs, careful not to be seen. As soon as he was able to move without fear of detection, he ran out the house and headed toward Miss Eliza's cabin as fast as his young legs could carry him. Once at the cabin, he banged on the door with all his strength.

"What on earth? What's wrong with you child?" Miss Eliza questioned as she answered the door.

"Soleil and Hope—they need help. Miss Vivian lost her mind. She got some man to come and snatch them up. She trying to make them disappear."

"Oh Lawd. Does Mr. Alex know?" Miss Eliza exclaimed, clutching her hand to her bosom.

"He's not here. Hurry, we have to help them."

"I'm coming."

Miss Eliza ran back into her house in search of a weapon of some sort. She grabbed her frying pan, and gave Joseph her rolling pin. Armed to the best of their abilities, they ran back toward the main house.

As they rounded the side of the house to the front, several distressing scenarios played out before them. In the distance, Soleil hung over the side of the large man's horse as he rode away at top speed. Vivian trailed not too far behind on her mare.

In front of them, a man attempted to put a feisty Hope into his wagon. She clawed at every inch of his skin, screaming for her mother.

"That's my girl," Miss Eliza cheered. "Let's go."

Joseph and Miss Eliza ran into the open, yelling and screaming as they descended upon the man. The attack was so unexpected he barely had time to defend himself. As he attempted to reach for his gun he released Hope, who immediately ran toward the house. Joseph saw him reaching and smacked his hand with the rolling pin.

When the man pulled his hand back in pain, Joseph shot his hand out and grabbed the gun from its holster. "Don't you move, mister."

The man raised his hands high above his head and froze in place, seeing the gun mere inches from his face. "Go on, take her. Just don't shoot me," he pleaded.

"You've got five seconds to get on your horse and ride away." Voice and aim steady, Joseph brokered no arguments.

Not willing to risk his life over a small child, the man did as he was told and made his escape. Miss Eliza and Joseph stood their ground, watching until the man could no longer be seen.

Once sure of his departure, they sighed with relief and hugged each other.

"Come on let's go check on the baby girl," Miss Eliza said.

"What about Soleil? We have to help her."

"She's gone, and we don't know where to. We have to wait for Mr. Alex to return. He is the only one who can help her."

Joseph knew Miss Eliza was right, but the need for action continued to plague him. Soleil was gone, and there was nothing they could do about it.

Alex could see the lights from his house in the distance. It struck him as odd for there to be so many candles lit this time of evening. The house was normally quiet around this time, as most of the staff had already retired to their own residences. Unease settled over him. He picked up the pace of his stride.

As he drew nearer, Alex made out the image of a figure pacing back and forth on the porch. Something wasn't right. Alex picked up his speed to an all-out run. The figure on the porch turned out to be Joseph, who immediately started running toward Alex as he emerged from the darkness.

"Joseph what happened?"

"Soleil is gone, sir. Miss..."

"What do you mean gone?" Alex bellowed, cutting Joseph off.

"Miss Vivian came and took her. She was going to tell you that Soleil had run away. There was another man that tried to take Hope as well, but Miss Eliza and I fought him off."

Fear and pain grasped Alex in a death grip, making it difficult to breathe. How could he have left her unprotected? How could Vivian be capable of such animosity, to steal the woman he loved from him? "Where is Hope now?"

"She's in the nursery with Miss Eliza. I don't know where Soleil is, but the man who took her was ugly as sin, tall, dirty looking brown hair and had a large scar 'cross his forehead."

The color drained from Alex's face. He knew of the man Joseph spoke of. He had a reputation of crushing the spirits and bodies of those brought to him. The thought of Soleil in his hands made him want to vomit. He had to hurry and save her. It would be a long ride to the beast's lodge, and so much time had already been wasted.

Alex ran to the stable, and without thought of a saddle mounted his horse. He rode into the night on the dark path, praying the animal would sprout wings.

Soleil sat quietly on the floor of the dirty cabin where the man had deposited her. *Think*, she told herself. She had to escape and find Hope.

Her abductor squatted in front of the fireplace, stoking the dying flames' embers.

The glint of something shining caught Soleil's attention. A knife rested on the table in the middle of the room. Instinct drove her as she raced to the table to pick up the knife, then lifted it over her head to slice down at the man.

Alerted by the stomping of her feet against the wooden floor, he turned and lifted his arm as she swung, causing her to nick his forearm. Before her hand had even returned to her side, his fist made contact with the side of her face, sending her hurtling toward the floor.

The skin on her cheek tightened as it began to swell. Blood flowed from the cut along her eyebrow. She couldn't move or even lift her head because of the pain slicing through her. Her vision was clouded by black spots as her eyes refused to focus.

Soleil wrapped her arms around her legs and drew them to her chest. Soft whimpers filled the room. "Alex," she murmured, "please help me."

She chanted the words over and over in her mind, willing Alex to hear them as she began to drift in and out of consciousness.

1859

"Alex! Alex, help me!" Soleil called out to her friend as she held the tree branch in a death grip. She chided herself for trying to compete with Alex to see who could climb the highest. Now she hung a good enough distance away from the ground that if she fell she would surely break something.

"Alex, help!"

"Don't worry, sunshine. I'm coming." True to his word, a few seconds later Alex descended the tree to sit on her branch. He straddled it and leaned forward, reaching out a hand to Soleil. "Take my hand. I've got you."

"I'm scared. I don't want to let go."

"Soleil, the angle of this branch won't let me lean far enough to get a good enough grip on you. I need you to reach out and

take my hand. Don't worry, I won't let you fall."

Soleil reached out a tentative hand toward Alex. Her arms were tired. Fatigue had set in to the muscles of her arms, which had carried her weight for too long. Her fingers strained to keep their grip on the branch. She reached out to Alex, but the distance was a little too far.

"Swing a little toward me."

"No! I can't," she whimpered.

"Yes you can."

Soleil tried again to reach out to Alex. This time she did as he instructed and swung her body. As their hands connected, Soleil lost her grip on the tree branch. Sweat made the hand she grasped Alex with slippery, and the force of her falling body caused him to lose his grip on her hand. Soleil braced herself for the pain that was to come when her body connected with the hard ground below. But the pain never came. Instead, Soleil felt Alex's arms wrapped around her as he shifted in midair. When they connected with the ground, Alex's body absorbed the force of the impact.

Soleil was a little dazed but otherwise unharmed. Beneath her, Alex gasped for air.

She rolled off him and began examining his body for injuries. "Have you lost your mind? Why would you jump out of the tree?"

"What other choice did I have? I couldn't very well let you fall and break your beautiful neck. As long as there is breath in my body, I will always protect you. Always."

Soleil's eyes flew open, the memory burning bright in her mind.

Alex. He had always been there for her, and always would be. Like the release of a dam, memory after memory returned to her. She and Alex hunting in the woods together during their youth. Her singing to Alex as they sat on the bank of a lake. She remembered them. She remembered everything. Each memory slammed into her heart, increasing the love she felt for him until there couldn't possibly be more room. As if her entire heart was filled with love for him.

She tried to lift her hand to hold her aching head, but the movement was blocked by thick iron chains wrapped around her wrists. The chains were staked to the ground, pinning her in place. Another set of chains were shackled around her ankles. Her eyes scanned the room. She was alone in the cabin's dimly lit interior.

The crunch of footsteps moving toward the cabin carried to her ears. Not wanting to alert him that she had awakened, Soleil closed her eyes and lay unmoving on the ground.

The poorly maintained door groaned in protest at being opened. Likely no oil had seen its hinges since it was installed in the cabin.

Though she feigned sleep, the man grabbed the chains attached to Soleil's wrists and hauled her to her feet. She gasped, stumbling to regain her footing. The man half-dragged, half-carried her to the back of the cabin, where he passed a rope hanging from the ceiling through the chains around her wrists. Then he grabbed the other end of the rope and hoisted her up, leaving her hanging from the ceiling with her arms above her head. He connected the chain around her ankles with a hook that protruded from the floor, leaving her exposed and making it impossible for her to move.

"Ready," the man shouted above her head.

The creaking door opened again as someone entered the cabin. Chained with her back to the door, Soleil couldn't see who the newcomer was, but her heart already knew.

"A chair, please," Vivian's voice spoke into the silence.

The man pulled a chair from a nearby table and sat it directly in front of Soleil.

Vivian sauntered around from the left and sat in the chair with all the grace of a lady during tea time. "Today you will learn your place. How dare you presume to be worthy of Alex's love."

"I dare because I am worthy. I am Soleil Jacqueline Dufor, daughter of Dominique Dufor, whose shipping company could rival—if not out-earn—Alex's plantation. Despite the hue of my skin, any man would be privileged to have my hand in marriage."

"Your memory has returned, I see. No matter. I will help you remember a new lesson today."

Vivian turned to the man. "I think ten lashes will do. Then I will take my leave, and you can do what you will with her."

Soleil wondered how so much hate could reside in someone's heart. Her only crime was loving Alex, and this kind of retribution was unwarranted. But she refused to beg this woman for mercy. She lifted her head and braced herself for the blows to come.

The man parted her hair and draped it over her shoulders and breasts. He took a knife and sliced her dress open from the dip of her back upward, pulling the fabric aside to expose her bare flesh. Soleil heard him step back to position himself for delivering the first lash.

No matter how she braced herself, Soleil was not ready for the whip's sting as it made contact with her flesh. Her cry of pain split the air. A brief pause followed, leaving just enough time for the sting of the first lash to subside before the second blow came, doubling the pain on her tender flesh. Soleil screamed in agony with each connection of the whip to her skin. She counted four lashes before the pain became too much and her world went black.

Chapter Thirteen

A SMALL FLICKER OF LIGHT shone in the distance. Tension eased from Alex's body at the sight of it. The agonizing scream of a woman pierced the air, sending shivers down his spine. He answered the scream with a guttural roar of pain and blazing hot rage. They would feel every ounce of pain they caused Soleil ten times over.

He spurred his horse into a reckless gallop. The stallion's chest heaved under the strain of the faster pace after their journey thus far, but Alex pushed him hard.

Alex listened for another scream, but he heard nothing. What if they had killed her? Fear gripped his heart. His clammy, sweat-slicked hands made it hard to hold the reins as the stallion careened through the darkness toward the cabin. Alex said a silent prayer that Soleil would not be dead when he found her.

Alex leapt from the horse before it had even stopped in front of the cabin. His heart pounded in his ears like the rapid beat of a tribal drum. He sprinted up to the tiny porch and burst through the door.

His vision clouded with murderous rage at the sight that greeted him. Soleil hung from the ceiling, arms bound by a chain, her head hanging limp as if in supplication. Her hair blocked her face from his view.

Vivian sprang from the chair she had occupied, backing away from him. He had been so focused on Soleil he hadn't noticed her until she moved.

Eyes wide, hands held high in surrender, her body trembled with fear under his vicious scrutiny. "Alex, I... I..." she stammered, "I did this for you. I wanted..."

Her words were cut short by Alex's open hand striking her across the face. Vivian stumbled backward as her hand flew to her reddening cheek.

Alex felt more beast than man in that moment, and was relieved he had been able to restrain his hand from becoming a fist. He had never raised a hand to a woman in his life. Vivian had been like a mother to him, which made her betrayal even harder to bear. "None of what you have done was for me. If you truly cared for me as you claim, you never would have struck at the woman who is my heart. You are to never set foot on my property from this day forward. If I see you again, I will not be so kind as to let you live."

As Alex spoke each word, he knew at the core of his existence that he meant each one of them.

As he glared down at Vivian, a door at the side of the cabin opened and a man entered carrying a bucket of water. The man looked from Alex to Vivian and immediately readied himself to attack. He threw the bucket at Alex's face and charged him.

Alex lifted his arms to deflect the bucket, leaving himself open as his attacker took him low in the midsection. They fell to the floor with the man on top of Alex.

As the man lifted his fist to punch, Alex flipped them, landing two punches to the man's face. The man bucked his hips, throwing Alex off him and quickly scrambling to his feet.

Alex stayed on the floor, clipping the man's feet from underneath him. The man fell back and hit his head against a wooden block. He lay unmoving on the ground.

Not caring if his attacker was dead or alive, Alex quickly got up and pulled the key ring from the man's belt. He unlocked the chains around Soleil's ankles, holding onto her as he unlocked the chains around her wrists.

She fell limply into his arms. He held her tightly to him. Shallow breaths passed through her lips, ruffling his shirt. He thanked God she was alive, and tried to coax her awake. "Soleil, please open your eyes for me. Please."

Her eyes remained closed, but she made a sound barely above a whisper. She repeated the whisper again. Alex bent his ear to her lips. He listened harder as she repeated the words over and over.

"*S'il vous plaît, pas plus.*"

Alex did not understand her words, but was glad she was able to speak at all. He gathered her in his arms and ran from the cabin without a second look back at Vivian, who still stood frozen, holding her face in shock.

It was hard mounting his horse with Soleil in his arms, but he managed and began the journey back the way he had come. He could not push the horse as fast as he had coming, but he kept him moving at a quick clip.

Instead of returning to his home, he guided the horse in the direction of Doctor Smith's house. It was late and he would probably be in bed, but Alex couldn't wait until the morning. There was so much blood, and he needed to know that Soleil was going to be okay.

Soleil remained semiconscious for the entire ride. Every so often Alex heard her whisper something in French, but could not understand what she said. When he finally arrived at the doctor's house, he dismounted, cradling Soleil in his arms as if she might break.

He ran up the porch steps and pounded on the door with his foot. A few minutes later a light appeared inside. The door opened to reveal a short, middle-aged man in his early fifties who appeared completely undisturbed by the intrusion.

Before Alex could even speak, the man stepped to the side and said, "Come in. Take her to the first door on the left."

Alex did as instructed. When he entered the room, it was plainly decorated with cream walls, a few chairs, and a small bed in the middle.

He laid Soleil in the bed facing him on her side, and pulled up a chair next to her. He looked down at her bloody and bruised body, hating himself. He had left her alone and vulnerable so he could go to a gala with another woman and socialize with people he hardly cared for. It was his fault she was in this bed.

The doctor came into the room with a tray of bottles, bandages, and medical instruments. He walked around the bed to the side opposite of Alex. He placed the tray on the side table and pulled up a chair. Alex watched as the doctor brushed Soleil's hair over her shoulder and parted the cut fabric of her dress to have full access to her wounded back.

He reached for a bottle and cloth from the tray and looked up at Alex. "I need you to hold her hands. I have to clean the wounds, and this will probably hurt her."

Alex did as the doctor requested, cursing himself that she would have to endure even more pain. As the doctor poured the liquid over her back, Soleil's face contorted in pain until she was finally torn from her unconsciousness.

She scanned the room, her eyes unseeing and wild and filled with abject terror. She snatched her hands from Alex's and tried to rise from the bed, shouting, "*Laissez-moi! Ne me touchez pas!*"

Alex held her down, which only made her fight more. "Soleil, calm down. You are safe. It is Alex. I'm here with you. You are safe."

Her eyes focused on Alex's face and confusion began to give way to recognition. She allowed him to lay her back down without protest. "Alex? Where am I?"

Alex stroked her un-bruised cheek and tried to keep his voice even and calm. "I brought you to a doctor. All is well."

Soleil looked over her shoulder into the smiling face of Dr. Smith.

"Hello, my dear. It seems you have been through a very rough night, and I am going to help you get better."

Soleil nodded and turned back to Alex. She allowed her head to melt into the bed's soft mattress before she gave into the pain, both physical and emotional, and wept. "I thought I would never see you again. Where is Hope?"

Alex rubbed her arm and held her hand again, offering what little comfort he could. "I will never let that happen. She is safe at home with Miss Eliza."

Dr. Smith resumed his work, wiping the blood from her back. She lay still for the most part, occasionally wincing in pain.

"The worst is over," the doctor said in a calming voice. "A few stitches and you will be fine. Alex, if you don't mind, would you step out while I finish up? It should not take long, but you look like you could use some air."

Alex hesitated, not wanting to leave Soleil's side.

She squeezed his hand in reassurance. "I am sure I am in good hands."

Alex rose from his seat and walked to the door. He could not bring himself to speak with all the emotions clogging his throat. Once outside the room with the door closed behind him, Alex leaned against the wall and sank to the floor. Knowing that Soleil was going to be all right, he finally gave in to the storm of emotions flooding through him and laid his head in his hands and wept.

Twenty minutes later, the doctor emerged from the room.

Alex wiped the tears from his face and rose to his feet. "Is she all right?"

The doctor placed a comforting hand on Alex's shoulder. "She is doing excellently. The amount of blood made the wounds look worse than they were. She only needed a few stitches and bandages for the rest. She is sleeping, if you would like to go in."

Alex shook the man's hand. "Thank you, doctor. And the reason..."

"That is none of my concern. I am here to heal those in need. I have known you since you were a young boy, and know you have a kind heart and would do her no harm. Now, I am going to salvage what little of the night remains. You are more than welcome to stay with her for the remainder of the evening. I will check on you in the morning, and if all is well, I will have my carriage take you home."

Alex thanked the doctor again and entered Soleil's room. The sheets had been changed and she now wore a soft, white sleeping gown. She still lay on her side and looked peaceful sleeping with her head on her folded hands.

Alex took off his boots and climbed into the bed beside her, cradling her head to his chest. The tip of her head rested just below his chin, and he could feel her warm breath on his neck. Holding her in his arms, he whispered into her ear, "I love you with every fiber of my being. I promise I'll never let you be hurt again. I will handle this entire situation. No harm will threaten you or Hope ever again."

After a final examination by Dr. Smith, Soleil was given clearance to travel home. Alex took the doctor's offer to use his carriage to ease the strain of the journey on her wounds. He was eager to get Soleil in bed and resting again.

During the entire ride home Alex held Soleil in his lap, cradling her in his arms as if she were a delicate piece of china. The doctor's care instructions ran repeatedly through Alex's mind, afraid as he was of forgetting even the tiniest detail. He would need to change her bandages later that evening, and he wanted to make it as painless a process as possible.

Alex looked down into Soleil's sleeping face. She had been in and out of sleep the entire ride. She usually only stirred when the carriage hit a bump in the road and disturbed her wounds.

He stroked the top of her head. He still couldn't believe that he had been blessed with such a gift. He did not deserve this amazing woman, but he would spend the rest of his life trying to be worthy.

As they neared the house, Alex saw a ripple in the curtains on the front window. A few moments later, Hope ran out the front door. She stood on the front steps, bouncing with pent-up energy.

As soon as the carriage pulled to a stop she was at the door, trying to pull it open. "Maman! Maman! Are you there?"

"Stand back, little one, so I can open the door. Then you can see your maman," Alex said with a gentle tone.

Hope quickly did as instructed, and Alex opened the carriage door and emerged carrying Soleil.

"Maman! Are you hurt?"

Soleil stirred at the sound of her daughter's voice. She reached out a shaky hand for Hope to hold. "I am fine, mon amour."

"You are hurt. Your face is hurt," Hope said, assessing her mother.

"Nothing that won't heal in time."

Hope shifted her uncertain gaze from Soleil to Alex. "Why is Maman hurt, Papa?"

Soleil opened her mouth to speak and shift the focus of Hope's question. "Hope, I..."

"No, it is fine," Alex interrupted, cutting off Soleil's response. "I will answer her question."

Accusation and pain radiated from the little girl's eyes as her gaze met Alex's. He would never harm a single hair on Soleil's head, but he understood her doubt after seeing her mother roughly handled at the hands of another man.

"You know Miss Vivian?"

"The mean lady who wanted to hurt me and Maman?"

Alex nodded his head. "Well, Miss Vivian was mad at your maman and me, so she wanted to punish us."

"Were you naughty?"

"In Miss Vivian's mind we were. You see, some people think I shouldn't love your maman because she has darker skin than mine. But I love both you and your maman with all my heart."

"What is wrong with her skin?" Hope gazed appraisingly between Soleil, Alex, and herself.

"To me there is nothing wrong with it. In fact, I think it one of the most beautiful things about her. Some people, however, don't think the way I do. But it is my job and your job to love everyone equally, no matter the color of their skin. And perhaps one day everyone else will also realize that there is nothing wrong with darker skin. Can you do that with me?"

Hope vigorously nodded.

"Good. Now let's get your maman inside."

Soleil watched the entire exchange between the two most important people in her life, and was struck speechless. The care Alex took in explaining everything to Hope touched the deepest part of her heart and soul. She would love this man until the day she died, with every fiber of her being. Even the tenderness he showed her as he walked with her into the house pulled at her heart strings.

When they made it to her room, Soleil was elated to be able to finally lay in her bed. The small interaction with Hope had nearly drained all her energy.

Hope climbed into the bed next to her mother and lay beside her with her small hand over her mother's heart.

"If you need anything, I will not be far," Alex said as he kissed each of them on the forehead.

Soleil was so exhausted, all she could do was make a small mewling noise in the back of her throat in response. Her eyes drifted closed before Alex had even left the room.

Chapter Fourteen

"IF I SPEND ONE more day in this bed, I might lose what little of my mind I have left," Soleil grumbled.

She had been confined to her bed for the past two days. Between Hope, Virginia, and Alex constantly hovering over her, she had yet to have a moment alone with her thoughts.

"Hush now. You need rest," Virginia chided as she adjusted the pillows behind Soleil's head. Her protruding belly pushed Soleil back into the bed as she leaned over her.

"I should be the one taking care of you," Soleil said. "You look ready to go into labor at any moment."

"I wish. This little one seems to be taking their time joining us in the world. I can't blame them, though: with free meals and never having to do for yourself, I wouldn't want to come out, either. Now lie back and don't complain, because we love you so much."

"Could you all love me in a location other than this bed?"

Virginia tossed her hands in the air in defeat. "I give up. I can't force you to heal. So stubborn. I'll tell Alex to come talk with you." With one last adjustment to the water pitcher and medicine bottles on the table next to Soleil's bed, she left the room in a huff of feigned indignation.

Soleil closed her eyes to revel in the momentary quiet. She peeked through the cracked lid of one eye when the door opened and heavy boots thudded against the floor. Alex had arrived.

He strode to the chair beside her bed that had been occupied by each of her guests as they rotated in shifts to watch over her. "I hear you are being a most difficult patient," Alex teased.

"Difficult is a matter of perception. From this viewpoint, you all are the difficult ones."

The hearty laugh that poured from Alex's lips cascaded over her nerve endings like an intimate caress. Soleil's breath hitched in her chest as the hairs on the nape of her neck rose to attention. She could bask in the joy of that laugh for the rest of her life and be content.

"I love you."

The words fell from her lips without thought. She hadn't intended to say them, but they burned in her heart so true they couldn't be contained.

Alex's eyes softened as he reached out and took her hand in his. "I know you do. I am so very grateful for that fact."

"No, I love you. You, as you are now. All that you are."

The confused look on Alex's face confirmed Soleil's suspicion that she was not properly conveying her feelings. Her mind stumbled through the task of matching her words with the swell of emotions churning through her. "I don't love you because my memory has returned. That only confirms I was right to give my heart to you. I don't love you because of the past. I love you because of who you are presently. Because of the man I now have the privilege to know. You pursued my heart relentlessly. You made me feel safe. You made me believe in something I never thought I could have. Thank you for loving me."

Alex cupped his hands around Soleil's face and lowered his lips to crush hers in a heated kiss. Soleil kissed him back, tentatively at first, until the fervor of her desire emboldened her enough to match the strength of his kiss. She tried to pour all the joy, longing, and passion he stirred in her from her body into his through their connected lips.

Too soon, Alex pulled back, breaking the sensual connection. His thumb grazed the sensitive skin of her lips as his loving expression roamed her face. "I have a surprise for you," he said with a silly grin.

For a moment, Soleil's mind stalled at the abrupt change in the mood and conversation. She wondered if she had imagined the heated exchange that had just taken place between them. But the feel of his thumb stroking her cheek reminded her it had been real. "Do you not think there would have been a better time to discuss such a thing?"

Alex released a jovial laugh from the depths of his abdomen. He pressed a quick kiss to her lips as the chuckles rippled through his body. "You very well may be right. But the surprise awaits nonetheless. I will send the ladies in, and they will help you prepare."

"Prepare? Prepare for what?"

"You shall see soon enough." With one last gentle kiss,

Alex rose to leave the room.

Hope, Miss Eliza, and Virginia stood on the other side of the door, barely giving Alex the chance to exit before pushing past him into the room. Their eyes sparkled with the delight of being privy to information Soleil didn't have.

"Would you like to see your pretty dress, Maman?" Hope chirped.

"My dress?"

"It looks like you get your wish. You may now leave this room. But first thing's first: we need to do something with your hair," Virginia said with a mischievous grin.

Soleil's heart soared. She glided down the stairs, feeling like royalty. Her gown was pale pink satin, reminiscent of the blushing petals of a rose. It hugged her waist before billowing out into a smooth bell shape that swept the floor as she walked. Ruffles adorned the off-the-shoulders bodice. Her hair was pulled back from her face, spiraling down her back in a waterfall of curls. An orange blossom wreath headdress with lace veil framed her head like a halo.

Her heart raced as the front doors opened. Heat that had nothing to do with the humid Alabama spring weather suffused her body. As she stepped onto the front porch, there he was. Her impossible dream.

Alex looked breathtaking standing at the end of the porch, waiting for her. Back straight, hands clasped behind him, chest puffed out, his entire lean, six-foot frame made a dashing display. The tailored Mulberry frock coat, cream waistcoat and lavender doeskin trousers accentuated the hard muscles he had accumulated from years of working on his plantation. His hair was swept back, allowing Soleil to see the burning desire and twinkle of joy in his eyes.

Tears stung the backs of her eyes as her heart overflowed with joy. Today she would be joined with him for the rest of her life. Smiles and tear-filled eyes greeted her as she walked toward Alex. Miss Eliza, Joseph, and many of Alex's tenants stood in a small congregation behind the priest. Charles stood to Alex's left with his arm draped around Virginia. Hope bounced on her toes as she clung to Virginia's skirt.

When Soleil stopped in front of Alex, he took her hands in his and kissed each of her fingers. "Do you like my surprise?"

"Very much," she said with a watery chuckle.

"Good."

Hand in hand, they turned to face the priest. His salt and pepper hair had been neatly trimmed. Crow's feet graced the corners of his eyes, showing that he was a man who enjoyed ear-splitting grins like the one he current donned.

He gazed between Soleil and Alex, then placed their joined hands on the Bible he held. "Today I have the privilege of taking part in something truly special. I will join together this man and woman in the bond of holy matrimony," he said, emphasizing the word holy. "The laws of this land may not recognize your union, but God does, and what he has brought together no man can tear apart. Repeat after me, Alex."

Alex repeated the vows the priest gave him. He promised to love Soleil through the good and the bad times. He promised to love and honor her. He promised these things until the end of his life. Soleil believed every word he spoke.

Soleil repeated the vows next. She spoke each syllable with conviction and an unwavering determination to see them through. She would spend the rest of her life striving to be her best. For Alex, for Hope, and for herself.

he gathered crowd erupted into cheers as the priest announced, "It is my pleasure to pronounce you Mr. and Mrs. Alexander Cummings. Go in peace. Thanks be to God."

Alex swept Soleil into his arms and kissed her passionately before all in attendance. The cheers grew louder with the occasional jest about how long it would be before the first babe was born.

Laughing, Alex turned to the crowd of people and said, "If I have my way, the newest addition to the family will be arriving nine months from the day."

"Yay!" Hope cheered. "I would like a sister, please."

The laughs from the crowd grew louder. Men came up to shake Alex's hand and pat him on the back in congratulations. The women flocked around Soleil, telling her what a beautiful bride she made.

Soleil looked at Alex. Her husband. From this day forth, they would walk through life side by side. Nothing sounded more perfect.

Soleil rubbed her shaky hands up and down the chemise covering her legs. Her stomach fluttered as she sat on the edge of her bed, waiting for Alex to enter the room.

They had hosted a small luncheon reception with those who had attended the ceremony. Food, wine, and hearty laughs were had in abundance by everyone there. A few guests had retrieved instruments from their cabins, and sounds of revelry issued late into the night.

Now it was time for her wedding night. The time when she and Alex would truly become one. Her nerves were wound so tight the sound of the door opening caused her to jump. She inhaled a deep, calming breath.

The gentle radiance of the many candles spread throughout the room cast a soft glow over Alex's features as he entered the room. The appreciation in his eyes as he admired the room made Soleil glad she had listened to Virginia when she said, "Believe you me, he will love them."

"Hello, my wife. My sunshine."

"Hello, my husband."

"I cannot tell you how I have longed for this moment. The day that I could call you mine. Your radiance far outshines the brightest star. I cannot fathom what I have done to earn such a treasure."

A warm flush spread up Soleil's neck and across her cheeks. "You're too kind," she replied, eyes cast to her clasped hands in her lap.

Alex placed his index finger beneath her chin and raised her face so their eyes met. Gaze never leaving hers, Alex reached out and tucked a strand of her loose curls behind her ear. "You have nothing to fear from me."

"I know. It's... I..." Soleil stammered. "I don't know what to do."

Alex gave her a reassuring smile as he took her hands and pulled her to her feet. "Just follow my lead." He leaned in until their lips were a mere breath apart. "May I kiss you?"

It was a small gesture, but Soleil understood. He wanted her to know that she controlled the pace of the evening. His lips hovered above hers, waiting for her permission.

"Yes," she said on a heady breath.

Alex closed the distance between them. His lips gently explored hers. He gave without demanding, allowing her the time to become familiar with his kiss. He hugged her to him, fitting her body perfectly against his. The kiss slowly transformed from giddy and excited to deeply sensual.

Soleil was so consumed by the kiss, she barely noticed his hand roaming up her back until the pain of her tender flesh shot through the haze of her love-addled brain. It was as if someone had thrown a bucket of ice water on her happy moment. She pushed on his chest, and Alex broke the kiss without protest.

"Are you well?"

"Yes and no," Soleil said before rolling her bottom lip between her teeth. "My wounds..."

"Did I hurt you?"

"No, but I don't want you to see them."

As if he could read her mind, Alex's expression softened. "You are the most beautiful woman I have ever seen. You are strong, and have persevered through many trials in a short period of time. Nothing could make me want you less than I do in this moment, or for the rest of our lives."

Alex bent his head and kissed her with all the love and passion in his body. He kissed her until she believed and felt in her bones that she was all he ever wanted. Scars and all. Soleil wrapped her arms around his neck, ready to love and be loved by her husband.

Alex cradled Soleil to his chest, basking in the glow of their lovemaking. He had never experienced such a bond or felt such intimacy with another human.

His hand stroked up and down her spine, replaying the experience in his mind until a memory caught his attention. "Soleil, while we made love I felt something that could not be, but I feel compelled to ask you. Have you been touched by another man?"

"No."

"How is that possible? You have Hope."

Soleil leaned an elbow against Alex's chest, propping herself to stare down into his eyes. "Hope is the daughter of my heart, but I did not give birth to her. She was conceived and brought into the world by a friend I lost, Abby. One night while Mrs. Williams was visiting some friends, James came by to visit her. He was drunk, but said he wanted to stay and wait for her to return. While Abby was out gathering kindling for the stove, he ambushed her and raped her. When Mrs. Williams returned, we told her what happened. She banned James from that day until she died. She thought herself a Christian woman, and as such could not allow further immorality to occur under her roof. Nine months later Hope was born, and Abby died during the labor. I have cared for Hope as if she were my own ever since."

"I don't think you will ever cease to amaze me. Taking on the responsibility of raising someone else's child. Your heart is so large I sometimes wonder how it fits in your chest."

"It fits perfectly fine, and even has room to grow. The bigger it gets the more love you shall receive, because I love you Alexander, with all that I am."

Alex's chest vibrated with his laughter as he pulled her face down to kiss her forehead, then her lips. "I am glad to hear it."

Chapter Fifteen

"**M**UST YOU DO THIS?"

"I want to do this. I want to proudly claim Hope as my daughter for all the world to see. I am not ashamed of her, or you."

"Then why am I not allowed to come with you?" Soleil pouted. She had quickly learned the power of a well-used frown, especially if it was tinted with a bit of sadness.

Alex kissed her forehead as he pulled her into his embrace. "It is my greatest wish that this hearing will conclude with little upheaval, but I cannot be sure. Thus I cannot risk your safety, or Hope's. Knowing you are with Virginia will give me peace of mind."

"As you wish, Husband." Soleil allowed her hands to linger as she adjusted the lapels of Alex's frock coat. Unease settled in her stomach and wouldn't leave her. She needed the connection, needed to be reminded of his realness. "I will wait however long it takes for you to come back to me."

The tension of the moment was broken as Charles rapped a quick knock on the bedroom door before entering.

"Well, that is a first," Alex chuckled.

"Are we ready then?"

"Yes, I will be right out."

"Thank you for your assistance," Soleil added. "And for letting Hope and me stay here. Please bring my husband back to me soon."

"I have no intention of doing otherwise."

Alex planted a soft kiss on Soleil's lips before following Charles out the door.

Alex strode into the hall, ready to get the hearing under way. Charles had pulled a few strings to get them an emergency hearing before a judge who would decide if the case would advance to a trial before a jury.

The cramped room was abuzz with chatter as townspeople filled the pews, awaiting the beginning of the session. No doubt they had not had a piece of gossip this juicy in years. Whispers of the case about the town's wealthiest plantation owner going to trial over the quadroon daughter of a former slave had spread like wildfire.

As he sat next to Charles, Alex saw the plaintiff, James Williams, stroll toward the table where his lawyer sat. At the last second, he changed course and came to stand in front of Alex. It took every bit of Alex's self-control not to drive his fist into James's smug face. He wanted to make the man pay for every second of worry and every ounce of pain he put Soleil through.

"I admit, at first I was just interested in the coin the pretty lady offered me," James said, "but now I'm actually curious to see how this all plays out."

Alex stiffened at James's insinuation. Someone had paid him to come after Hope, and Alex had a feeling he knew who. "To which lady do you refer?"

"Well she said she was your fiancée, but I guess she was lying. Came to me blubbering about how she needed help keeping you from the clutches of Soleil's voodoo spell or some such nonsense. Like I said, I just wanted the coin she offered," James said as flippantly as if he were talking about the weather. With that, he turned his back on Alex and took his seat next to his lawyer.

Once Judge Lloyd had entered and taken his seat, Alex knew this was not going to be an easy battle. The deep scowl that cut his eyebrows into his forehead showed he wanted to be anywhere other than here, presiding over this case. His shrewd eyes peered over the rim of his spectacles as he looked between Alex and James. "I understand we are here on the matter of a quadroon girl named Hope. The plaintiff, one Mr. Williams, alleges that the girl is his apprentice and was taken without his permission. Let's hear it, then."

James's lawyer scrambled to his feet. "Yes, Your Honor. The child's mother, one Soleil, was the former slave of Mr. Williams' mother. After the passing of the 14th Amendment, Soleil was unable to care for herself or the child, and thus stayed on to work for Mrs. Williams. As you well know, per state law, being found a vagrant or without employment is prohibited for the recently freed blacks. So upon his mother's death, my client graciously allowed Soleil's employment to continue, and took Hope on as his apprentice. Also as per state law, an apprentice is not allowed to leave their master's employ until the master grants such permission. Mr. Williams did not grant such permission when Soleil absconded with Hope late in the evening a few weeks back. Now he is requesting that Hope be returned to his care as the law states she should be. That is all, Your Honor."

Judge Lloyd listened intently as the lawyer gave his dry speech. Once the lawyer resumed his seat, his gaze shifted to Alex and Charles. "Whatever you did to make enemies with the plaintiff was a mistake on your part. This case is a sham and I can see it a mile away. However, the law is on his side. Unless you have a very compelling argument, I am inclined to grant his request. So what do you have to say?"

Charles stood to address the judge. "Your Honor, Mr. Williams has no claim to Hope now, because he should have never had claim to her in the past."

"I'm intrigued. Go on."

"The child's mother is a citizen of France, and was born as free as you and me. She was abducted on her sixteenth birthday and wrongfully sold into slavery. According to federal law, the condition of the child follows the condition of the mother, and as her mother should have been free, so should the child. Moreover, all legal rights to the child, enslaved or free, belong to my client, as he is her father."

The room erupted into a hive of noise as the spectators gasped and buzzed with the news just revealed. To publicly claim a child of African descent was unheard of. Yes, the fair-skinned children roaming some plantations were a glaring beacon of what transpired between white men and black women, but this declaration pulled back the rug, revealing the dirty secrets underneath.

"Order! Order. Quiet down," Judge Lloyd demanded, red faced, as he banged his gavel to be heard above the roar of chatter. "Order I say, or you will be removed."

The room immediately quieted; no one wanted to be removed and miss a single second of what was to come.

Judge Lloyd snatched his glasses from the bridge of his nose as he leaned forward, boring a hole into Alex with his hard gaze. His blotchy red face was the model of righteous indignation. "Listen to me carefully, boy. If you go down this path it will not end well for you. Is this how you wish to proceed?"

"It is," Alex declared, unwavering.

"Then you leave me no choice. This case is dismissed, as the defendant has full rights to the child in question. However, I must now bring new charges against you. You have openly admitted in court to engaging in acts of fornication, and more disturbing, you engaged in these acts with a Negro woman. For this crime, you are hereby sentenced to three years of hard labor to be served in the state penitentiary. The Negro woman in question is to be apprehended and serve the same sentence. Take him away."

Again the audience broke into a frenzy of excited chatter. Some cheered, while others hurtled insults at Alex for being so audacious as to mix his blood with the African animal.

Alex shot to his feet, rage and fear surging through his body in a storm of emotions. He looked to Charles, who sat open-mouthed and stunned. Neither had seen the possibility of this outcome.

Charles snapped back to life as a guard converged on them, ready to drag Alex away. "Alex, I am sorry."

"There is no time for that. Protect Soleil. Get her to safety. It is time to implement our contingency plan."

With a curt nod, Charles left to do what needed to be done.

Alex didn't struggle as the guard shackled his wrists and led him away. Everything would be well in the end. He had to believe in that. Charles knew what to do.

Alex lay on the cot in his cell, staring into the darkness. He was the only occupant of the building's three cells, leaving him with utter silence and his thoughts. Worry over Soleil and Hope made sleep impossible. He trusted Charles with his life, but he would give anything to have confirmation that his girls had made it to safety. In the morning he was to be transferred to the penitentiary, and his heart longed to see Soleil's beautiful face once more before he left.

The crunch of dirt and gravel sounded from below the window of Alex's cell. "Alex? Alex my love, can you hear me?"

Alex came to attention as the soft voice reached his ears. Was he dreaming? It was impossible for him to be hearing what he thought he heard.

"Alex, please answer me."

"Soleil?" Alex crossed to the tiny window to hear her better. It was too high for him to see her, but the mere sound of her voice was like a soothing balm on his aching soul.

"Yes! Alex, I..." Her voice broke on a sob. "I'm so sorry. This is all my fault. I should have returned to France and left you to live your life in peace."

"Soleil, what are you doing here? Charles had specific instructions to get you to safety."

"I know. We are to leave at first light, but I couldn't go without hearing your voice one last time."

"It isn't safe for you here. You need to leave now."

"I know," she said with a weary sigh. "I just need you to know that I am sorry. And that I love you so much."

Alex rested his head on the hard wood of his cell wall. He closed his eyes, imagining he stood before Soleil. "You have nothing to be sorry for. I would do it all again, given the opportunity. To have been your husband for even a day was the greatest gift this life has ever given me. I want you to..."

Shouts and screams in the small jailhouse cut off Alex's sentence. He walked to the bars of his cell to lean against them, listening intently to the commotion going on in the front of the jail house.

Fire! Men shouted the word repeatedly as their heavy footsteps raced through the building. A closed door separated the front of the building from the holding cells, making it impossible to see what was happening.

At first he saw nothing, but then the yellow glow of the burning flames roared to life as they squeezed beneath the bottom of the closed door, then climbed the wall.

"Help! Help! Release me," Alex shouted.

No response greeted him. Not even the sound of footsteps. The building had been evacuated of its inhabitants. All but him. Soleil's frantic voice reached his ears.

Alex ran back to the tiny window. "Soleil, move away from the building."

"What is happening? I see smoke rising from the building."

"There is a fire. I believe the guards have all fled the building."

"You are there alone? I will get help."

"No! Go find Charles. If you go around the front and they are there, they will arrest you. Please do as I say."

"Alex, please! Don't you dare leave me."

Alex could hear the agony in each word she sobbed. His heart filled with sadness. Not for himself, but for the fact that he wouldn't be there to comfort Soleil through the dark time ahead.

Heat licked up the back of his body as he stood flush against the wall. The flames had journeyed into his cell, consuming everything in their path. Sweat burned his eyes as it poured down his face. "Soleil, I love you!"

"No! No! No! Alex!" She sobbed.

"I have always loved you."

"Alex! Alex! No! No!" Tears ran down Soleil's face as the roaring flames consumed the tiny wooden structure before her eyes.

"Soleil, I love you!"

"No! No! No! Alex!" She sobbed.

"I have always loved you."

Those were the last words she heard before the flames burst through the tiny window of Alex's cell. She fell to her knees and rocked back and forth with her arms wrapped around herself. Pain like she'd never known ripped her beating heart from her chest and crushed it underfoot. Sobs tore through her body as she screamed her agony into the night sky. The world around her began to spin until finally everything went black.

Chapter Sixteen

ISS ELIZA STARED DOWN at the letter, eyes wide and mouth hanging open. It had been read to her three times already, but she still couldn't believe it. It was either the cruelest joke or the greatest blessing.

"Read it one more time," she said handing the letter back to Joseph.

"The words haven't changed I promise you," he retorted. But despite the roll of his eyes in exasperation, the boy did as he was told.

To Miss Eliza Smith,

I hope this letter finds you in the best of health and prosperity. My name is Charles Willcox, Esq. And I am the executor of the estate of the late Mr. Alexander Cummings. I offer my deepest condolences to you and yours over the tragic loss. He was a dear friend to my family as well. I write today on behalf of the estate to inform you that in his last will and testament, Mr. Cummings decided to provide an inheritance for you and your family before his untimely passing. He left instructions that his property was to be divided equally among all those listed under his employ at the time of his death. You will be provided half an acre of land, as well as, five-hundred dollars a year for the next seven years. Mr. Cummings hoped this gift would allow you to find prosperity and independence in his absences. At your earliest convenience, I request that you come to my office to sign the necessary documents to accept your inheritance.

Yours truly,

Charles Wilcox, Esq.

As Josephs words trailed off Miss Eliza sat hunched in her chair, hand clutched to her chest as tears fell silently down her face. She had known Mr. Cummings was a good man, but never could she have imagined such a fate would befall her. Tears of joy over the gift, mixed with tears of sorrow for the poor man and the broken-hearted woman he left behind.

"Thank you, Joseph. Now listen here," she said, sternly pointing a finger in his direction. "Mr. Cummings was a good man. What happened to him is a true tragedy. But he left us a gift most people would never see in their lifetimes. It's our duty not to squander that gift. You are going to take yourself to school every day and get your education. You are going to do amazing things and be an upstanding gentleman. You will grow into a man he could be proud of. Understand me?"

"Yes ma'am," he replied. Face stern Joseph gave a curt nod of his head in acceptance of all that Miss Eliza and Mr. Cummings called him to be. He would be a man they could all be proud of.

Soleil sat in front of her easel as she had done every morning for the past week. It sat in the corner of the apartment's tiny room, next to the lone window. Light filtered through the dirty glass, casting a freckled pattern over the canvas. From below, hoof beats clomped on cobblestone, and New Yorkers' carried on their daily lives with boisterous voices.

She lifted the paint brush and held it suspended in the air. Yellow paint flowed over her fingers, trailing down her arm and dribbling drop by drop onto the skirt of her dress. She couldn't bring herself to place the brush on the canvas. It fell from her hand as she let her arm fall limp at her side.

Soleil folded in on herself, grabbing her head in her hands. She rocked back and forth in her chair on the balls of her feet. Visions of fire burned through her mind's eye. Reds, oranges, and blinding yellow light haunted her every waking moment. Soleil lifted her head to look at the other canvases strewn across the room.

Scorching flames and charred remains dominated each picture. Rage, fierce and powerful, swelled in Soleil's heart with each passing second. An agonized wail thundered through her trembling body and trumpeted from her mouth. Giving in to the fierce storm within, Soleil grabbed the frames one by one, slamming them against the wall, the floor, tearing the canvases to pieces.

Soleil stood, chest heaving, in the aftermath of her destructive outburst. Her anger ebbed, making room for heartbreaking sadness. She preferred the anger; the sadness left her feeling helpless and alone.

"Alex. Alex. Alex." She chanted his name like a sorrowful prayer.

"Maman? Are you well?"

Soleil wiped the tears from her eyes, struggling to regain

her composure. She never wanted Hope to see her this way. To see her so broken. "Come here, *mon amour.*"

Hope ran to her mother's outstretched arms and wrapped herself in Soleil's embrace. "I miss Papa, too," she whined.

"I know, *mon amour.* I know." Soleil rubbed the little girl's back to comfort her. Hope needed her. Even though she barely had the strength to continue breathing, she needed to dig within herself to be strong for her little girl. "Will you do your maman a favor and go help Mrs. Virginia with the baby while I clean up in here?"

"Yes, Maman." Shoulders slumped, Hope walked out of the room.

Once the door closed behind her daughter, Soleil walked to the full-length mirror to assess herself. Dark circles framed red-rimmed eyes swollen from days of constant crying. Her unkempt hair was overrun with knots and tangles.

Although her nose had gone numb to her bodily odors, Soleil was sure her stench could rival the smelliest barn. She had not washed in days. She couldn't remember the last time she had eaten. Her haggard appearance screamed at her that it was time to heal. Time to pick up the broken pieces and assemble them into the shadow of a happy life.

"You look much better." Virginia cradled her nursing son as she greeted Soleil with an encouraging smile. His little mouth suckled greedily.

Charles Edward Wilcox II had been born three days before, a healthy, squalling bundle of flaming red hair like his mother.

Even through the pain, Soleil's heart had instantly expanded to give him a special place.

"I feel much better."

"Soleil, I..."

"No." Soleil cast her eyes to the ground, running her hands down the front of her skirt to gather her resolve. "The time for talk of death and sadness is over. I need to look ahead to the future, not to the past. After all, we sail for France tomorrow."

"I can't wait! I'm so excited. It's like a brand new adventure."

"You and Charles do not need to come with us if you do not want to. I know you are worried for me, but your world cannot revolve around mine."

"Have to? We want to! There is nothing for us here. Besides, I get to travel to London, spend my summers in Paris. I plan to fill my wardrobe with enough of the latest Parisian fashions to make any high-class debutante green with envy."

"Thank you."

Virginia placed a reassuring hand over Soleil's. "I consider you a sister, you know, and I love you as such. We will make it through this together."

"Yes. Yes, we shall." As she said those words, Soleil realized she believed them. She would make it through this dark time with the help of the loving people around her.

Soleil inhaled a deep breath. Cleansing, salty air filled her lungs. The large dock was alive with the sights and sounds of ocean life. Seagulls cawed overhead. Men and women called out to loved ones disembarking from nearby vessels. Soleil held tight to Hope's hand as their small party moved through the sea of passing strangers. She was bumped by the occasional shoulder of someone squeezing through the crowd.

Muscles tense, her eyes roamed the crowd, constantly scanning the faces of those she passed. The large crowd and tight confines made her uneasy. As they neared the vessel that would carry them across the ocean to her homeland, she reached into her reticule to check on their tickets yet again.

"Pardon," a man yelled, his stout body pushing past Soleil. His shoulder connected with her chest, nearly toppling her to the ground. The small purse flew from her hands into the throng of moving feet.

"Are you hurt, Maman?"

"No, mon amour. But I dropped our tickets. Please help me search for my reticule."

Soleil and Hope crouched low to scour the ground, but there were too many moving legs blocking their view.

"Excuse me, miss. You seem to have dropped this."

Every cell in Soleil's brain ceased functioning as the smooth baritone washed over her. Her body went rigid, every muscle drawn taut, leaving her frozen in place on the busy dock. Had she heard what she thought she'd heard? Or had her mind finally plunged into the realm of insanity? She pivoted slowly on the balls of her feet to face the voice's owner.

"Alex." Soleil's hand flew to her gaping mouth. Here he stood before her. The man who gave wings to her soul. Soleil sucked in choppy gulps of air. Her breath hitched as uncontrollable sobs overtook her trembling body.

"Hello, my sunshine."

Everything around them ceased to exist. Soleil ran to him and wrapped her arms around his neck, holding tight and never wanting to let go. She rained kisses over his face, not caring about the spectacle they made.

"Papa!" Hope squealed, wrapping her little arms around his thigh. "You're here, Papa! How are you here?"

Soleil pulled back from Alex's embrace as Hope's question broke the joyous fog surrounding her brain. "Yes, how are you here? You died. You made me believe you died." Hurt colored the elation she'd felt just moments ago.

Alex pulled her back in. "I'm sorry, I honestly didn't know the fire would happen. It was a part of Charles's plan to free me."

Soleil looked at Charles and Virginia, who stood a few feet away, watching them. Charles wore a triumphant grin, while Virginia looked as shocked as she was. Soleil found a little solace in the fact that she wasn't the only person left in the dark.

"When I knew what was happening, we needed to make sure it was safe before I could return to you. There was no body, so we wanted to make sure they didn't search for me and follow me back to you. I couldn't risk your safety, or Hope's."

Soleil understood his need to protect her, but it still stung. She had spent the last week mourning him and the life they could have built together. She had known no greater pain than thinking she would have to continue through this life without him. "Did they search for you?"

"For a time. Then they gave up and concluded I had died in the fire, and my body had turned to ash."

"What about your plantation? If you are assumed dead, what will happen to your people?"

"I divided my estate among them and established a trust to pay their wages for a few years. I gave it all up. There is no cost too high for me to pay to have you and Hope. Do you forgive me?"

"Yes," Soleil answered. Despite the hurt, if nothing else she had learned that life from one second to the next was not guaranteed, and she wanted to cherish each and every one of them. She would not waste her energy creating wedges between them.

Alex lifted her in his arms and kissed her passionately for all the world to see. Hope bounced and cheered next to them. Placing her back on her feet, Alex took hold of her hand in his left and Hope's in his right. "Come. Our new home awaits."

Epilogue

"PUSH, MA CHÉRIE. ONE last big push."

Soleil did as her mother instructed, pushing with all her might.

"Good! Look who we have here."

Soleil lay back on her pillows, exhausted by the labors of childbirth. Through the haze of pain, she could hear her child wailing, full of life. Soleil held out her arms for the precious life she had just brought into the world.

"Your son is beautiful," her mother cooed as she held the crying babe.

Soleil took the crying infant from her mother's arms and was filled with pride and love. He had ten tiny fingers and ten tiny toes. A mop of black curls spiraled around his perfect head. His long legs kicked out from beneath the blanket, and she knew he would be tall like his father.

She thought back on all the hardships she had faced in America, and felt blessed to have this little miracle in her arms. He was the beauty that arose from all the ugliness.

It felt good to be home, with her mother beside her while she brought him into the world. A feeling of homecoming had washed over Soleil upon her arrival. When she saw her parents for the first time in over six years, Soleil could not stop crying or let them go. They sat holding each other for what seemed like an eternity. Finally, she remembered Alex and Hope standing next to her, and introduced them to her parents. Imani and Dominique welcomed their new son-in-law and granddaughter with as much love as they had their daughter.

While they talked and caught up on what had happened in each other's lives, Soleil learned that her mother and father had stayed in America for a year after she had disappeared. They had looked for her from sun up to sun down. After a year of searching and with no new clues to her whereabouts, they returned to France, heartbroken.

In the time since their arrival in France, Alex had taken over her father's shipping company under Dominique's guidance, while Soleil had taken over the duties of the house and helping her mother. That is, until she went into labor this morning.

After the birth was finished and everything was cleaned, Alex and Dominique entered the room with Hope on their heels. Alex watched as his son slept peacefully in his mother's arms. He walked over and sat next to her on the bed, kissing them both on the forehead.

"You have a fine son. He will grow in a strong young man," Dominique declared with pride as he wrapped his arm around his wife's waist.

"That he will," Alex replied. "We shall have to send word to Charles and Virginia so they can visit."

"We will take care of that for you. Rest and enjoy your new son. We will return later," Imani said, before ushering her husband out of the room.

Hope climbed up onto Alex's lap and reached out to stroke her baby brother's cheek. "He looks so wrinkly."

Alex and Soleil both laughed. "Well, he has been floating around in Maman's tummy for a long time."

"Will he stop looking so wrinkly?"

"One day, yes. He will be chubby and cute," Soleil responded.

"Good. But I still love him as he is."

Alex bent down to kiss his daughter's forehead. "I am glad to hear it. You have a heart as large as your mother's. I must say, I never thought I could fall in love yet again, but I fear I have done so with my son. He is beautiful, and I love him and his mother for giving him to me."

Soleil smiled up at her husband. She loved him with all her heart, and now she needed nothing more.

The End

Dear Reader,

Thank you so much for purchasing this book. I hope you enjoyed reading Soleil's story as much as I enjoyed giving it life. The Cost of Hope is the first book in the series about Soleil, her family and friends.

If you finished and thought, "I need more!" you are in luck. Simply click this link (https://www.gscarr.com/forum) to be transported to my website where you can join my book lover's community. There you will find a copy of the deleted chapters of how Soleil and Alex met in their youth and what happened when she was abducted. Moreover, you will get to hang with me and get sneak peeks of my WIPs.

Oh, and while you're there don't forget to cast your vote on whose story you would like to see next, Virginia & Charles or Imani & Dominique. I don't do newsletters because I think if the average person is like me then they never check their email anyway. And I'm on social media, but I really stink at it and trying to figure out algorithms and the like to make sure you hear from me is not my idea of fun. So, if you ever want to chat with me and the rest of the crew to gush over the story, the royal wedding, if lunch meat is really meat, or ask me any other random questions, the forum is where to do it.

Also, I learned a lot of very interesting information re-searching for this book. Below is a list of some of the sources I used to breathe life into this story. If you are interested in learning more about life and laws in the post-Civil War south, I encourage you to check them out.

Richter, Jeremy W. "Alabama's Anti-Miscegenation Statutes: A Short History of Anti-Miscegenation Statutes." Jeremy W. Richter, 20 June 2017, www.jeremywrichter.com/2017/05/05/anti-miscegenation-statutes/.

Costly, A. (2018). Southern Black Codes - Constitutional Rights Foundation. [online] Crf-usa.org. http://www.crf-usa.org/brown-v-board-50th-anniversary/southern-black-codes.html [Accessed 18 May 2018].

Novkov, J. (2017). Segregation (Jim Crow). [online] Encyclopedia of Alabama. http://www.encyclopediaofalabama.org/article/h-1248 [Accessed 18 May 2018].

Again, thank you so much for reading! And I will see you in the next book.

~G.S. Carr

About the Author

G. S. Carr is the writer of the debut novel The Cost of Hope, which is was a finalist in the 2018 RWA Romance Through the Ages contest. Ms. Carr can normally be found locked away with a good book in her home in Charlotte, NC or traveling the globe to places like India, Bali, Tokyo, or London.

CPSIA information can be obtained
at www.ICGtesting.com
Printed in the USA
LVHW090535051218
599324LV00002B/542/P